L.A. Blues III:

Five Smooth Stones

L.A. Blues III:

Five Smooth Stones

Maxine Thompson

www.urbanbooks.net

Urban Books, LLC
97 N18th Street
Wyandanch, NY 11798

ISBN 13: 978-1-60162-391-1
ISBN 10: 1-60162-391-7

First Mass Market Printing August 2013
Printed in the United States of America

10 9 8 7 6 5 4 3 2 1

Distributed by Kensington Publishing Corp.
Submit Wholesale Orders to:
Kensington Publishing Corp.
C/O Penguin Group (USA) Inc.
Attention: Order Processing
405 Murray Hill Parkway
East Rutherford, NJ 07073-2316
Phone: 1-800-526-0275
Fax: 1-800-227-9604

L.A. Blues III:

Five Smooth Stones

Maxine Thompson

Then (David) took his staff in his hand, chose five smooth stones from the stream, put them in the pouch of his shepherd's bag and, with his sling in his hand, approached the Philistine.

—1 Samuel 17:40

Dedicated to the memory of my mother, Artie Mae Vann, who was one of the best mothers in the world, under the worst circumstances of oppression, racism, and poverty.

Chapter One

Newport Beach, California

We saw what you did with that decapitated head. If you don't want to go to prison doing life for murder one, or as an accessory to murder, I suggest you get that money to us.

Oh, no! The nightmare was starting all over again. I'd memorized the last text message, one of a half dozen, which had come over my iPhone earlier that morning, and it kept replaying over and over in my mind like an old, warped vinyl record. Clearly, I was being blackmailed by a person or persons unknown. My question was: what was going to be my next move?

"Chop, chop! Move it! We're ready to shoot." The loud voice of Vince, the reality show's director, interrupted my train of thought.

"Lights, action, roll it!"

Feeling detached, I looked on as the tattooed-up cameraman clapped his hands in a syncopated rhythm. With a flourish of hand motions, he ordered everyone to get into formation and act out their assigned roles in what my reality costar, Haviland, was touting on Facebook, Instagram, and Twitter as "The Wedding of the Century." Her wedding was taking place on a ten-story yacht, *The Hail Mary*.

This was her televised marriage to her live-in boyfriend, Trevor, which would be part of our reality show, *Women in Business*. The TV audience just ate up her crazy antics. Haviland was psycho, but underneath it all, she was loveable, I had to admit.

We had already filmed all but the last three shows for the first season, and we had a chance of being signed up for another season, which we were all excited about.

"Move over," the cameraman barked. He waggled his camera, holding his hand like a hatchet, telling me to move over. As the sun blazed down on me, I scooted closer to my Latina foster sister, Chica, who was the matron of honor, while, I, as a single woman, was a bridesmaid.

Chica's husband, Riley, was one of the groomsmen.

"It's getting hot," Chica whispered under her breath.

I could see Chica's olive skin tanning to a deep bronze, so I knew I must have resembled burnt toast about now. We were standing so close I could smell her breath, which smelled like mint.

I hoped she couldn't smell the vomit residue on my breath.

"I heard that," I agreed between clenched teeth. "I'll be glad when they do the real ceremony and get this thing over with."

"Oh, come on, will you, Trevor!" Control-freak Haviland's snarl rose above the din as she snapped at her new husband-to-be in one of her famous meltdowns. Face set in a grimace, arms akimbo, she continued, "This is my wedding day! Why do you have to eff up everything? Get a move on it."

"I'm sorry, dearie." Compliant, Trevor stepped into place as neatly as a sheet being snapped before being spread on a marine's bunk bed. "What's wrong with you now?"

"Oh, really, Trevor?"

Everyone in the audience leaned forward, eyeballs peeled, ear hustling. The tirade was about to begin, but the minister stepped in and tactfully smoothed over it. "Marriage is a sacred bond and union. We have to compromise. Love covers a multitude of sin."

"Oh, no, she didn't," Chica hissed.

"SMH," I said in text-speak for shaking my head. "Cussing at the altar."

Chica and I glanced at each other out of the corner of our eyes and shook our heads in unison.

"This is some ratchet mess already," I said sotto voce. In a swift move, I pulled my fist to my mouth, just in time to keep from vomiting. *I guess that's what I get for gossiping.*

"What's the matter, *mija*? You look a little green around the gills." Chica leaned in, apprehension creased on her brow.

I shook my head, as if to say that I was all right. However, I wasn't feeling well at all.

Something about the way the canary sun slashed onto the ocean waves and the seagulls cried out to each other in a keening sound made me nauseous. A flock of ravens formed an arrow in the sky and made me think of another one of my mother Venita's sayings: "a bad omen." I thought about the black bird, which flew into my garage apartment yesterday and shuddered; another bad sign.

I struggled to hold my composure as I looked on at the crowd of one hundred people gathered for the nuptials. I really wasn't feeling up to Haviland's histrionics today, but the camera was eating up this social peccadillo. If anything, they were calling Haviland "the breakout star" of our reality show because of how she bullied around her fiancé, soon-to-be husband. The sad thing about it was, I felt Haviland's words would set the dynamics for their upcoming married life: bi-racial Haviland would be bullying her Caucasian husband-to-be, Trevor, who acted as the compliant victim; Haviland, starring as the sadist, and Trevor, as the masochist. He gave the term "lily-livered" new meaning, just as Haviland took the term "bridezilla" to a new level. Moreover, she'd been PMSing all week, and her nose flared out in the fashion of a bull's because she was spazzing so. For whatever reason, Trevor had decided to tie the knot with crazy Haviland after two years of living together "in sin," as Haviland now called it. I'd never seen such a nasty-acting wife-to-be, but Trevor seemed to love her dirty drawers all the more.

We had already marched in twice, but had to reassemble for this new, hopefully last, camera shot. The cameramen descended the area like a swarm of sea rats. Numb, I took my place in line in the bridal party and plastered on my public smile. We had to give the impression of this so-called wedding being unscripted. Except for the actual wedding ceremony, this was our third take. My smile, my everything, including me, felt fake. I felt as if I'd had a plastic surgeon make a mistake around my lips, they felt so frozen.

There was a side of me that almost wanted to jump out of my skin and off the yacht that we were on in celebration of Haviland's fourth wedding at thirty-two—actually she was thirty-four, but in Hollywood women lowered their age.

"Take three," the director called out.

Haviland's wedding was seen as a cachet for our reality show. Although we still had more shows to shoot, this would be the finale show of our first season.

What am I doing here anyhow? I kept asking myself over and over. I was so queasy; all I wanted at that moment was to be at home in my bed, near the safety of the commode. I also needed to be near my laptop in order to figure out what to do about whoever my blackmailer(s) was.

Whoever it was had already text messaged me five times before this last message. At first, I thought it was a prank. But when they e-mailed a picture of me in the Santa Monica park, dumping the wicker basket that contained Tank's butchered head, well, I knew these people meant business. I know it sounds stupid now, but I had to get out of the country to Brazil in order to save my brother's life. I didn't have time to call the law and possibly be detained for questioning. I just left an anonymous tip on a payphone.

Out of loyalty to Haviland, instead of being at home now, I was on a yacht, swaying back and forth on the ocean, and it took all my strength to keep from barfing all over the deck. I was so nauseated just the very thought made me swallow the scorching vomit, which hit the roof of my mouth in a splash. *Uggh*. The moment passed because we were finally slowing down. We'd just pulled off from Newport Beach and were about twenty miles out at sea.

As far as I was concerned, I was fighting the worst case of nausea in history, but I tried to stand tall as the bridesmaid. Chica, matron of honor, and her other six bridesmaids, including me, were all wearing short Vera Wang ecru-colored bridesmaid dresses and matching peau de soie shoes.

Haviland, the star of the show—I mean this ostentatious extravaganza—was wearing crepe satin and a French Chantilly lace gown made by Carolina Hererra. The dress had 152 buttons along the back and was fashioned after the gown from the movie, *The Twilight Saga: Breaking Dawn, Part I.*

Since she was her own wedding planner, Haviland had selected a Victorian theme for her wedding. Everything had to be perfect.

Don't get me wrong. I was not jealous of Haviland, but I couldn't be happy for her, either. I couldn't help but think, *This should be me marrying Romero.* When he asked me to marry him, I should have married him, instead of running off to Rio to free my brother, Mayhem, from his abductors. Why didn't I realize that Romero was the best thing that ever happened to me before it was too late? Now he was gone forever. I wanted to stop by the cemetery and talk to him after the wedding. That was the only way I could feel close to him ever again.

Why was I here you might ask? *Because everyone expected me to be strong and to keep it moving.* They didn't care that I just lost Romero, the love of my life. If my arm wasn't hanging off me, with torn tentacles exposed, gushing blood, people thought I was fine. They expected me to be the strong black woman.

Just as the yacht was ten stories high, everything was over the top. Haviland always had to do it up large. I had to give it to her. As one of the best in the business of wedding planning, Haviland had a fastidious eye for detail. You could see it in the impeccable choice of fabric. Her Victorian theme threaded throughout, from the floral arrangements of calla lilies, to the white tablecloths trimmed in a thin thread of gold, to the six-foot ice sculpture shaped like doves, the fountain with Cupid squirting out mimosa from a curlicue penis, and the fake Roman columns wrapped in gold garlands, which flanked the decks. Yet I was so depressed; nothing looked beautiful. Everything had a dark cast to it.

"We are gathered here today . . ." The minister—a medium-height bald brother who, according to the program, was named Reverend Edgar Broussard—spoke in a solemn tone.

I was feeling so lousy, I blanked in and out. *Come on with it already,* my mind screamed. I needed to go to the restroom really, really bad.

"I promise to love and honor and obey," the minister intoned.

Absently, I listened as Haviland said her vows.

"I promise to love and honor." Haviland cleared her throat and purposely dropped the "obey."

Chica and I glanced at each other and suppressed smiles. *Haviland is a fool.* We were betting this marriage would have the lifespan of a tsetse fly. How these two managed to live together over two years was beyond me.

"I now pronounce you man and wife."

Hallelujah! I thought. *Next, pit stop to the bathroom.*

"Cut! It's a wrap," the director called, using hand signals. All this brought it back to me that this marriage getting its start under the glare of the Hollywood lights was mad crazy unbelievable—another bad omen, as far as I was concerned.

Everyone stood up and began clapping. The good news for Haviland was that she and her Jewish adoptive mother, Irene, had reconciled. She was overjoyed that Irene and her extended family members were all present at the wedding.

For the first time in several years, Haviland had been clean for the last two years, and now that she was making a comeback in her career, her mother couldn't be happier. She'd never stopped loving Haviland; she was just burnt out with the numerous drug rehabs.

Irene, along with two dozen of her adoptive parents' relatives and friends, were sitting in the front row of the family section. Since her adoptive father had passed, her adoptive Uncle Morty walked her down the aisle and gave her away.

The family and friends began taking pictures with their iPhones, instagraming, and tweeting right away. In addition to that, Haviland had a professional crew to take photos of her wedding.

In the tradition of Haviland's Jewish heritage, the newlyweds stamped a long-stemmed champagne glass. "Mazel tov!"

In honor of Haviland's Black heritage, they also jump-ed the broom. Next, the family of the bride and groom went up to the fourth story of the yacht to take "photo ops," as Haviland liked to call them.

On the real though, this was not a happy day for me. Two and a half months ago, I'd just buried Romero, the first man who taught me how to love. Inside I was grieving, yet, at the same time, I was furious. How could Haviland plan this rush wedding, knowing I was in mourning? I felt the same way a widow would feel. But I went along with it, since she took such good care of my pet ferret, Ben, while I was in Brazil, trying to free my brother from a hostage situation. I owed her big time.

I hated to remember my ordeal—how I went to Brazil to free my brother, Mayhem, and how it ended up bringing me into the hellish space I was in right now: pregnant by either my lover or a rapist from when I was drugged while in Rio. Geez! I had no way of knowing, although my suspected perp, Alfredo, said he didn't have intercourse with me, but who knew? I didn't have a rape kit at the time to test.

I didn't think I could do a DNA test because Romero was dead. I didn't know his relatives, and I definitely didn't want to do a test on his daughter, Bianca. I also couldn't go back to Brazil and get a test done on Alfredo. The real reason I didn't want to face a DNA test was I didn't want anyone to know I was raped.

By the time I made it back to the States, Romero got killed in a shootout trying to free my kidnapped brother and, the truth be known, I lost it for a while. When I came back to my senses, I found out I was pregnant. If I knew for sure it was Romero's baby, I still would have had a hard time because I had never thought about having children, but under these circumstances, I just didn't know.

Abortion was still legal, thanks to Mitt Romney not getting into office, and I'd been contemplating my options, but time was running out. I'd be approximately twelve or thirteen weeks on Tuesday. Today was Saturday. A sense of trepidation rose up in me. Why had I waited so late? In theory, I've always believed in a woman's right to choose if she didn't want to have a child, but I never knew what I would do if I was faced with an unplanned pregnancy.

I felt bipolar most days. I was being torn from two different sides. I believed a child had a right to life, but I also believed in a woman's right to choose.

How could I even think of having a child? I was not mother material. I was not married. My private eye business was just taking off. I was beginning to get clients from Bel Air and Beverly Hills. Our reality show was blowing up. Where would I fit in a baby? I fed my face and I had fed my family. Period. That's all I'd known for thirty-five years. How could I ever change and be responsible for another human being?

I didn't want to bring a child into a life where he didn't feel he had any choices—that he was a victim, which is what I've had to fight all my life not to be.

I had so many what-ifs. What if the baby was fathered by that monster Alfredo who might have raped me? But what if the baby was Romero's? *What should I do?*

Chapter Two

Now that the charade of a wedding ceremony was over, I marched out in formation with some unknown groomsman, Trevor's best friend, Peter, or whatever his name was. As I speed-walked down the aisle, I felt someone's eyes boring into my back. I turned when I made it to the end of the aisle and noticed the minister staring at me. *What was that all about?* I wondered, but I rushed on, trying to make it to the bathroom.

Chica, close on my heels, followed me to the luxurious restroom as my heels clicked on the mosaic tile. I couldn't hold back the wave of nausea any longer, as I squeezed my hand over my mouth and regurgitated.

I made it to one of the empty stalls just in time to vomit into the toilet like the little girl in *The Exorcist*. Head hung over the toilet bowel, knees on the cold marble floor, I retched and retched and retched some more. A typhoon had moved inside my stomach and would not let up until it hit the back of my throat, then gushed out into the commode. This cycle repeated itself over and over and over. As a slew of green lava rushed out my mouth, I could hear Chica's voice calling behind the closed stall's door.

"*Mija*, what's wrong with you?"

I heaved and heaved until just a frothy foam trickled out. I finally came up for air. "I'm okay." I gasped helplessly between breaths as I stood up and leaned my forehead against the stall's cool slab of granite.

"What do you mean you're okay? You don't sound okay to me. Z, are you sure you're all right?" Chica called from outside of the bathroom as she banged on the door.

Gagging air with nothing left on my stomach, I tried to catch my breath. A string of saliva ran from my mouth and I wiped it with the back of my hand. Between breaths I said, "It must be something I ate." The truth be known, I hadn't eaten anything but a little broth that morning. This was my meal from yesterday.

Finally feeling some relief, I sat down and urinated since I couldn't help from peeing all the time, it seemed. I came out the restroom stall, washed my hands, then rinsed out my sour mouth. The next thing I knew Chica grabbed me by the shoulders, spun me around, then peered deeply down into my eyes.

"You look funny." She shook her head and pursed her lips the way she did when she was figuring out something. "You sure you aren't pregnant?"

"No." I averted my gaze as I threw the paper towels into the waste bin.

In turn, Chica grabbed up a paper towel, scurried into the bathroom, got on her knees, and scrubbed up the floor where I'd missed the toilet. She came out the bathroom, paper towel crumpled in her hand and shaking her head. She washed her hands and let them air dry. "Z, stop lying," Chica snapped. "You're pregnant, *mija*. I've had five babies. I should know. I thought you looked different. It's something about your eyes. That's how Shirley knew I was pregnant with Trayvon."

For the first time in months, Chica could talk about her murdered fifteen-year-old son, Trayvon, without breaking down crying. She was talking as if this was a warm memory—her getting pregnant for the first time at eighteen by a drug dealer, Dog Bite. Memories; how time softened tragedy.

As I felt hot tears swim to the surface, I shook my head to clear my eyes.

Chica reached over and hugged me, her tone as soothing as brook water running over smooth pebbles. "Why are you hiding it? You're a grown-ass woman. Girl, won't that be nice to have Romero's baby? You really loved him. This way, you'll always have a piece of him."

I bit my bottom lip, fighting back the tears, which floated dangerously near the surface at all times these days. I noticed that tears were becoming my daily friend. I wasn't used to this rollercoaster of emotions. One minute I'd be all right, the next I'd be sobbing uncontrollably. Finally I spoke up. "I'm not sure if I'm going to have this baby."

Chica caught her breath. "Wait a minute. What do you mean? Are you saying what I think you're saying?"

I nodded.

"Please don't do it." Her voice was adamant, almost pleading.

"I just can't have a baby right now . . . not ever. I don't have a motherly bone in my body. I'm too scarred emotionally. When I was eight years old and my mother had my brother Diggity, I changed his diapers and got up at night with him so much, I think I knew then I'd never want babies. She just handed him over to me like I was the mother."

Chica glanced around the bathroom, stooped down, peeked under the other stalls to make sure we were alone, then went into the bathroom and pulled out some toilet tissue. She handed it to me. "I'm going to tell you something I've never told another soul."

"What?" I wiped my eyes, and gazed out. Chica looked like I was seeing her through a rainy window since my eyes were so bleary.

"When I was out on the streets, just before I got clean, I got pregnant by one of my johns. I didn't know who the father was and I went and had an abortion . . ." She paused, as if it was too painful to remember, let alone put into words.

"And?"

"On that first day everything seemed okay, but the next day, I started hemorrhaging. I wound up in the hospital in ICU. While I was passed out, they gave me an emergency hysterectomy in order to save my life. At the time, I was just happy to be alive. I never dreamed I'd clean up and find a good man like Riley so it was just another day in the life of a crack head. But now, I'd love to have a baby for Riley and I can't ever give him one. "

"Does Riley know about this?"

"He knows I've had a hysterectomy, but he doesn't know why. I heard what you said about dick is not your friend."

"When did I say that?"

"When I wanted to tell Riley about my being molested as a child. You said something like, 'Don't tell men all your dirty secrets.'"

"Right. Save that for your girlfriends."

Chica gave me a serious look. "You're more than a friend. You're my sister." Then she added, "It'll all work out. Trust me."

She pulled me into a long hug and was saying some more soothing words about her helping with the baby, which sounded more like Charlie Brown's teacher, "Wonk, wonk, wonk," as far as I was concerned. I heard Chica's voice washing over me, but I didn't feel comforted. Between the nausea, the constant peeing, the fist tightness in my womb, the sore tingling in my growing breasts, I was miserable all the time. I pulled away and rushed out the restroom. I couldn't tell her the truth about the possible rape in Rio. I still didn't know what I was going to do. I found a table and I sat alone.

The dinner choices included grilled Cajun salmon, chicken cordon bleu, or Cornish hens with wild rice, asparagus, and a Greek salad. Dessert consisted of the most decadent piece of black forest cake slathered with a dollop of whip cream and the largest scrumptious Bing cherries I'd ever seen, but I knew I couldn't hold it down so I didn't try.

An example of Haviland's fastidious attention to detail was demonstrated in the impeccable calligraphy on the menu. I just picked at my food so my stomach wouldn't get upset again. I was thinking about what Chica said. Would I regret having an abortion?

"Hello. Why are you sitting over here by yourself?" A strangely familiar voice interrupted my thoughts.

I turned around and found myself face-to-face with the minister. He wore a white starched collar like a priest and a black old-fashioned Nehru-styled suit.

I glared at him, throwing all the shade I could muster up. "Why not?" I just wanted to be left alone.

His face melted into genuine lines of concern. "You seemed troubled."

"No, I'm good." I waved my hand in a "get lost" gesture.

"I didn't mean to disturb you. I've got to leave, but there was something about you. I'd like to give you my card, just in case you need prayers. You're welcome to come visit my church, too."

I looked down at the small business card. *Fellowship Baptist Church, Inglewood, California. Reverend Edgar Broussard.* I slid the card in my purse next to my Glock, which was licensed, and which I carried with me at all times.

"I hope to see you again." He gave me a tentative look, as if he expected me to say something in response.

"How are you getting back to the shore?"

"I'm taking the ferry back. I've got to get to work. "

"What kind of work do you do?" I leaned forward with interest.

"I'm a fireman."

"A minister who works?" I lifted my eyebrow in an incredulous manner. I didn't mean to sound sarcastic, but a working minister was an oxymoron in my world. I'd seen all the big churches on TV and splattered throughout Los Angeles. My relationship with organized religion had been like that of a relationship with a distant cousin since I became grown. I think the last time I stepped foot inside a church was at my nephew Trayvon's funeral. Shirley made us go to church so much after I went to live with her as a foster child at the age of nine, I really made a vow that when I got grown I'd never go to church.

"You know Apostle Paul and the disciples were tentmakers," Reverend Broussard said. "They worked when they weren't out making disciples. So I follow in their footsteps. Besides, not all of us have mega churches."

"Oh, so you're not one of the pimps in the pulpit?"

The minister paused. "If that's what you want to call them. I could take offense at what you're saying. I know there are some bad ministers out there, but I try to live by the Word. I fall short sometimes, but I do my best."

I didn't respond to him.

"Well, I must be getting along."

I wanted to tell him I didn't want to hear anything about any old God or any Christianity.

But most of all, I was angry at God. I almost wanted to shake my fists at the heavens and scream, "What next, God? You're doing a good job up there. First, *You* take my family from me when I was a child, then You kill off my first true love, and now I'm pregnant with a baby that may or may not be my lover's child. What else you got good for me, God? Is that all You got?"

I silently made a vow. *I promise to find the two men who kidnapped my brother and indirectly caused Romero's death. I will get to the bottom of this if this is the last thing I do.*

I knew whenever I made a vow, I followed through with it.

I wanted to tell the good reverend I didn't want to hear anything about any old Jesus or any Christianity. If there was a God, why was I born into the life I was born into—with my mother being a Crip, my brother Mayhem being a Crip, or, the coup de grâce, my father being murdered in front of my eyes when I was nine years old? How could I not be scarred? Give me a break.

As everyone got up to do the Cupid Shuffle from the movie *Jumping the Broom,* I remained seated. I looked on as the dances evolved into the Wobble, the Electric Slide, and the Dougie. The women outnumbered the men ten to one, so it was good they had the line dancing going on. The party was getting heated up. I thought about how well Romero and I used to salsa together and a pang of loss hit me again. I sipped my water slowly to keep from regurgitating again.

Gradually, my stomach began to settle down. Instead of dancing, I was enjoying myself with a bottle of water, and finding solace in my settled stomach. One day I would be happy; the next, I'd be miserable. Little things, such as not feeling sick to the stomach, made my day now.

Even water tasted good, now that it wasn't coming back up. I didn't want to go into the main ballroom and sit on the dais with Haviland and the wedding party because if I got sick again, she might guess. Up until now, I hadn't told either Chica or Haviland that I was pregnant, but Chica seemed to have guessed from my vomiting. However, I didn't confirm or deny my pregnancy when Chica asked me. I trusted Chica not to say anything; we'd held each other's secrets since we were raised together in foster care. But I didn't want big mouth Haviland to know—particularly if I terminated the pregnancy.

To begin with, I was not the motherly type. Never wanted children after being a foster kid. Truthfully, I was afraid I wouldn't know how to be a good mother.

What would I do with a baby? But then I got down to the heart of it. What if the baby wasn't Romero's? Could I raise a rapist's baby?

One day I would be okay; the next, I'd be miserable. I'd even driven to an abortion clinic, not once, but twice, but the protesters surrounding it scared me off the first time, and the second time, I just sat in my car and cried.

First of all, let me explain something. It wasn't that I was religious or anything that stopped me each day. Maybe I didn't want to be seen on the Internet or Instagram where someone snapped me on the camera going into the clinic. Don't get me wrong. I'm no saint because of the reality show. I really don't know what stopped me.

In all my thirty-five years, I'd never been pregnant. For one, I didn't even think I could get pregnant, since I'd been sexually active more or less (meaning I had periods of celibacy, particularly when I first got sober) since I was nineteen. I've been married twice, once where the marriage was annulled. I'd been single the last ten years. I generally used condoms, but the last time I was with Romero, he didn't use one. I was drugged in Rio, so I don't know what happened while I was out, but I do know I was tampered with downstairs in my cootie-cat.

After being raised as a foster kid, even though I had a good foster home with Shirley and Chill, who were still my surrogate parents, I was leery of risking motherhood. As far as I was concerned, Venita, my biological mother, pushed us out into the world with no more concern than a cat has for kittens and we all wound up spread to the four winds. I had no role model of how to raise a child, other than the care my foster mother, Shirley, had given me. But, was that good enough to be a mother? But then I got down to the heart of the matter. What if the baby wasn't Romero's? Could I love that child?

I cut my iPhone back on, but the signal was weak. Within minutes, my phone vibrated. A text message came across: I see where you put out a call on Facebook and Twitter for a biological sister named Righteousness. I think I might be that person.

For a moment, everything around me fell silent. The world froze like children playing the game Red light/Green Light. I had to stop reading I was so floored. I sucked in a deep breath, gathered my wits about me, and continued to read the message.

Hello, my name is Rachel Jackson . I saw your call on Twitter and Facebook for a female child born in Sybil Brand Institute in L.A. in 1986 named Righteousness de la Croix. I think I might be that woman . . . I now live in Ypsilanti, Michigan. You can call me at 734-999-1111. I was adopted at age ten through "Wednesday's Child" through Fox 11 KTTV in Los Angeles. I am available in the evenings.

She'd also sent an attached picture of herself. Right away, I could see some of my mother Venita's features. Although she was what some black people would call a "redbone," this Rachel had Venita's cherry nose and slanted eyes.

I text messaged back: You look like my mother. Let's talk at 9:00 tonight. I will call you. I'm at a wedding on a ship. I can't call you from here.

Okay, she text messaged back.

I was so excited, I forgot my unwanted pregnancy, I forgot my nausea, I forgot my black-mailer, and I almost forgot where I was. Years melted away and I was still nine, worrying about the basketball in my mother's stomach, which I later learned was a baby sister, who somehow survived when my stepfather, Strange, beat the mess out of my mother when she was seven months' pregnant. I was so excited I couldn't wait to catch the next ferry going back.

I made my way over to the dais where the bridal party was seated. The line of well-wishers had thinned out and the newlyweds were surrounded only by their wedding party. I was supposed to have sat at this long table with Peter, but I had elected to stay in the dance hall. I'd missed the first dance of the newlyweds.

"Z, where have you been?" Haviland snapped petulantly. "You missed the throwing of the bouquet and the garter."

"I'm sorry, but I got a little seasick." I caught myself, then changed the subject. "Girl, you're looking radiant." I blew air kisses, a Hollywood habit I'd picked up from Haviland.

Haviland was beaming, her makeup still intact. You could see how happy she was being the center of attention. She was the cynosure of all eyes, and, as an actress, she really hammed it up. Even so, she had this determined look like this was it, like she might make it through her fourth marriage. For her sake, I hoped so.

"Thanks for sharing our day," Trevor said.

"I wish you both all the happiness," I said sincerely. "I'm leaving, Haviland, Trevor."

In spite of Haviland's protests regarding me leaving the reception so early, I insisted I had to leave. I hugged them both, in the best mood I'd been in since the wedding started. They were due to fly out for Paris for their honeymoon later that night.

"Have fun. Congratulations!"

Chapter Three

Absently, I twiddled and twirled my ankh, which I wore around my neck, as I sped up the 73 West Freeway toward L.A. in my rental SUV. A few months ago, a Santeria had given this amulet to me when I was in Rio. Sometimes this ankh brought me comfort and lifted my mind from fear. I was still wondering if the ankh was what gave me the power to kill four men by myself when I was surrounded in Brazil.

Driving along, in a moment of clarity, I felt a sudden urge to go to an AA meeting, but I wanted to go to a meeting with people who looked like me—brown. Plenty of AA meetings were scheduled in Orange County, but I wanted to go to one in L.A. I'd been sober for almost three years now. Up until Mayhem was kidnapped, life had been good— brand new because of my newfound sobriety.

It hit me that I hadn't been to an AA meeting in almost three months but, fortunately, with this pregnancy and the constant nausea (which I was kind of hoping both would magically go away), drinking was the last thing on my mind. I thought

about it. A meeting wouldn't hurt. It always
gave me clarity about a situation: how should I
handle the reunion with my long-lost sister? I
wouldn't talk about my unplanned pregnancy, or
my reunion with my sister, but generally, I'd hear
a solution in what was said by one of the people
who opened up and disclosed more.

I merged from the 405 Freeway to the Harbor
Freeway, exited at Vernon and was driving down
Vernon to Vermont in South L.A., all the time
my mind was on my baby sister. So, her name
was Rachel now. What would she be like? Would
she remember me? I last saw her when she was
about eight or nine and living in a foster home in
Rowland Heights.

My mind drifted back to Romero. I decided
I would go to the cemetery tomorrow and put
flowers on his grave and talk to him about my
situation. *Should I abort this baby?* My real question: *Romero, is this your baby I'm carrying?*

*Oh, no! I don't want to be on some Maury
Povich TV show with the DNA test.* I could see
the drama now. Would his family come forth and
say, "That's not Romero's baby. He doesn't look
anything like him—I don't care if he is dead!" *Oh,
Lord!* And Romero came from a crime family
background, too.

My mind wouldn't rest. I couldn't stop thinking about this pregnancy. To take my mind off
my dilemma, I thought about my sister, Ry-chee,

aka Rachel. I had told her I would call her back at 9:00 P.M. It was only 6:00. I had time to make an hour AA meeting in the hood.

I was so excited about going home to sit down and really talk to my baby sister, I wasn't as conscious as I usually am. Wahoo-wahoo. Suddenly the wail of numerous sirens swooped down into my consciousness. Loud sirens blared around me, and a cordon of police cruisers were zooming down on me. My heart catapulted in my chest.

For a moment, I thought the law was after me for disposing of Tank's head. Were these the two agents who came to me with the proposition in the first place? Had my blackmailers turned me in since I hadn't gotten them any money?

I held my breath, waiting for the squad cars to stop and pull me over. Instead, the black-and-white squad cars whizzed by me in a blur, sirens screaming, horns blaring, tires screeching. I drew a deep sigh of relief.

Oh, Lord, somebody was going to pay for the mess they made of my life.

Then, out of nowhere, I saw what looked like green leaves filling the air. I thought it was some type of green snowfall, which, either way, would have been strange in L.A.

Everything seemed surreal. I could see greenery floating in the air, a whirlwind of verdant-looking leaves. Onlookers rubbernecked and came out to see what was going on. People swarmed out into the streets, screaming, dancing, hollering, jumping, leaping, as if they had the Holy Ghost.

What's going on? I wondered, regarding the commotion. People, bent over like cotton pickers, lifted what appeared to be leaves up off the street. The total bedlam reminded me of the 1992 L.A. riots. Was the sky raining leaves? Then it occurred to me. This was money! This was more absurd. The sky was raining money!

A police on a bullhorn barked, "People, put that money down. We have you on tape. You will be arrested for obstructing a police investigation. These men are armed, reckless, and considered dangerous."

As they gathered up the money, people were oblivious to the police orders. More trails of people came flooding from their houses to pick up the dollar bills. Cars stopped while the drivers and riders craned their necks out the window to see what was going on. A throng of young men wearing hoodies in honor of the murdered black teen Trayvon Martin had gathered in the street and was picking up money. Pandemonium reigned and everything seemed bizarre.

The police continued to roar in a stentorian tone over a horn. "People, go in your house. You are obstructing a police pursuit. Get out the way! We have you on camera! If you pick up any of this contraband, you will be arrested."

I could see all this purloined loot being picked up, and, oddly, I felt a strange sense of exhilaration. A sense of justice. As if somehow a wrong was being righted. I knew I'd never do it, but for a mother with five kids to feed, no job, and no food, maybe this was moral. Right and wrong sometimes shifted in the kaleidoscope of harsh reality.

"Money, money, money," people chanted, dancing wildly up and down the curb and onto the sidewalk. "It's raining money!" Some threw the money in the air.

In the manner of the old Martha Reeves and the Vandellas song, people were literally dancing in the street. Several people threw up their fingers in gang signs. Some were doing the Crip walk to a rhythm with a made-up song that went something like, "Kiss my ass, popo!"

"Fuck you, pigs!"

"Go to hell, motherfuckers!"

I kind of figured out what was going on, and there was a side of me that cheered the robbers on. I know it was wrong, but a perverse side of me was hoping that they got away.

"It's Robin in the hood!" someone quipped.

Bam! A loud noise exploded. The car the police pursued suddenly crashed into a truck.

I guessed the robbers were caught because farther up ahead, as I was stuck in traffic, I saw the police squad cars surround the speeding car. Guns were drawn. One man seemed to get away, but the other suspects surrendered.

Mesmerized, I started pulling over, trying to get out of the way of the traffic. I cut my radio on to see if I could find out what was really going on. Before I could get a news station, and while I was watching what was going on, out of nowhere a car barreled down on me like a bulldozer, and there was another bam!

I started twirling into a dervish-like spin, and the whole time I was crying, "What is happening? Help me, Lord!"

The next thing I knew I was turning over like a tumbleweed. The collision caused me to flop over and over again. After what seemed like an eternity, the SUV stopped and turned upside down like a turtle on its back.

"Help me, God!" I cried over and over again.

I had my seat belt on and, strangely, I didn't budge. I didn't move out of my seat. When I tried to unbuckle my seat belt, I was stuck. My air bag had blown up, but it also kept me penned in my car. That's when I began to panic.

For a moment, the world went black.

Chapter Four

Carjackers? was my only thought as I drifted back into consciousness.

With my senses returned, my neck lurched, and a pain shot up my back. Obviously, some car had hit me. That much I knew.

After I don't know how long, a tapping started at my window. I heard a strange female voice calling into my car, "Roll down your window. Miss, are you okay?"

I let my window down, and this angel stuck her hand in the car and held my hand.

"Help is on the way. I called 911 on my cell."

Drowsily, I wondered if I was imagining this stranger. Was she another angel in my life? She reminded me of how Romero saved my life from a gangbanging group of wannabe rapists when I was eighteen.

The lady talked me through the accident as she popped up into my peripheral vision. "I took my car and blocked your car so no one else would plow into you. I tried to get the driver's license plate but whoever it was was moving too fast. They had dark windows so I couldn't see in the car either."

My eyes swamped in tears of appreciation. "Thank you, miss."

All of a sudden, I could hear the drone of what sounded like an emergency crew, paramedics, maybe even helicopters. I don't know how much time elapsed as the woman talked to me in a soothing voice. I must have sunk in and out of consciousness because I looked up and saw a fire truck parked near my car. Through a fog, I could hear sirens in the distance. I heard a familiar voice, which had a rich timbre to it.

"Ma'am. Are you hurt? "

I looked up—which was actually down since I was upside down—and a fireman wearing a black shirt with an orange and white triangle badge on the sleeve was kneeling down with his hands splayed on the ground, talking to me in a calm voice. It sounded strangely familiar.

"Miss, don't cry. You're going to be all right. Are you hurt?"

"I'm hanging upside down. What happened?"

"It looks like a hit and run," I heard someone say.

Although my eyes were kind of blurry and I was still in shock, somehow, I recognized the voice. It was the minister's who had just married Haviland! "Aren't you Reverend . . . Edgar . . . the minister who officiated over Haviland's wedding?" I said haltingly. My voice sounded strange since I was still hanging upside down.

"In the flesh. Reverend Edgar Broussard. What happened?"

"A car hit her and kept going. She flipped upside down," the lady Samaritan was explaining.

"What?" I asked drowsily. The world was spinning and I was dizzy.

Silently, I thanked God I'd added insurance to the rental I was driving. I hadn't wanted to drive my hooptie on the freeway to Newport Beach and I'd taken out the accident insurance, just in case, so that was covered.

"How did you get here?" I asked Reverend Edgar.

"Remember, I told you I had to leave for my shift. I took a ferry back to land."

"Small world." Then a pain hit my shoulder where my seat belt had cut into my skin with the impact.

Everything happened in a blur after that. I felt like I was at the bottom of a well as I heard the buzz of the Jaws of Life as they sawed me out my seat belt and out of my car. Somehow they lifted me out the car, plopped me on a gurney, and deposited me in an ambulance. Racing through the streets, sirens blaring, the ambulance took me to USC hospital, which used to be old County General, since I didn't have health insurance. I was waiting for my Obamacare to kick in since I was self-employed.

It reminded me of when I was in the hospital after Romero's death. I woke up, strapped down to a hospital bed, sore from my fight with four men to the death in Brazil, worn out from a shootout with Mayhem's kidnappers, and forcefully anesthetized because of my screaming about Romero's death, but alive.

I guessed I was still alive now, which is always a good thing.

Earlier this year, when I was at the Academy Awards posing as a reporter when I was actually doing an investigation on a missing starlet who was believed to be a victim of a black serial killer known as the Grim Sleeper, an FBI agent, Special Agent Jerry Stamper, and a DEA agent, Special Agent Richard Braggs, took me into custody. They told me I had to go to Rio to get marked money that Mayhem's girlfriend, Appolonia, was allegedly holding for them or they would kill him.

Let me recap. Before I left the United States, I had helped get Mayhem's three sons out of L.A. with my mother, Venita, acting as their guardian/grandmother to keep them from getting killed. I'd run all over the nightlife of L.A., looking for clues as to who had kidnapped my brother. Before I left, I stopped by our office and received a basket in the mail with Tank's decapitated head. I left the head in the park, so I could get gone to Rio to get the money that I assumed was ransom money for my brother's kidnapping.

While in Rio, I learned about a surviving African religion and its voodoo power. A Santeria had worked her magic over me, gave me an ankh, which I still wear, and sent me out to free Mayhem's girlfriend, Appolonia, from this cartel. I didn't free Appolonia, because she didn't want to be freed, but she gave me the flash drive for the money. Afterward, I escaped by coming up the Amazon River.

The two agents, Agent Braggs and Agent Stamper, met me at the LAX airport, demanding the money I had access to, but I refused to give it up until I got my brother released. I told them for us to do the exchange at Venice Beach.

To my surprise, Romero showed up at the Venice Beach Pier. Bullets began flying everywhere and he got killed during the shootout that freed Mayhem. After that, everything was such a harrowing wild ride, I hadn't gotten in touch with how I even felt about the whole fiasco.

After Romero died, I was out of it. I hadn't even talked to Mayhem since the shootout. If Chica and Haviland hadn't pulled me through the shooting of our reality show, I'd still be lying in bed, ensconced in my grief. The two would show up at 4:00 A.M., before it was time to go on the set, and literally help me shower and dress. Each day I put one foot in front of the other, I must have gotten stronger. That's how I wound up at Haviland's wedding.

Chapter Five

I was lying in emergency with an IV in my arm and some type of machine attached to me that hummed along, but I had no idea what it was for. Smells of human life, blood, feces, pain, suffering, and antiseptic assaulted my nostrils. I thought about a few years ago when I got shot in the line of duty on the LAPD, and how it felt waking up after surgery. At the time, I didn't know if I was in this world or the next. This time, though, I felt like I was going to be all right.

"You're going to be all right," Reverend Edgar said, reassuringly patting my hand.

"Thank you so much for helping me." My voice reminded me of how I used to sound when I was drunk before I went to rehab two years ago. My words stumbled out in a slurred iambic tetrameter.

"I've got to get back to work. I put your purse on the side of your bed. It was in the car, so you've got all your ID."

"Okay," I murmured. I checked and my gun was still in there. It was inside a pink case.

I must have dozed off. I woke up thinking of this minister/fireman who had just left my bedside.

"That was nice of him," I mumbled drowsily. I couldn't get comfortable as I tossed and turned. I wondered if I was bleeding so I checked for my blood and didn't see any—only bruises on my arms and legs.

Blood made me think about the six men I had killed—ironically, all in my new line of duty as a private eye. Funny thing was I never killed anyone when I was on the LAPD. In each case, as a private eye, it was down to me or them, though. I cringed. *That still leaves their blood on my hands. What will I say on Judgment Day?* But what if I killed my baby?

Ironically, I canceled the two appointments I'd made at an abortion clinic. Now that I thought I was about to lose the baby, I couldn't stand the thought of a miscarriage. For the first time, this baby was more than an inconvenience. It was a life . . . a life inside of me. Maybe my baby was still alive . . . I reached down into my underwear and pulled out my hand to examine it. I wasn't bleeding. I thought I would've been bleeding if

I'd lost the baby. I let out a sigh of relief, then dozed back off. I think they'd given me some type of sedative.

I woke up again as they were rolling me on a stretcher to a regular room where I wound up being alone. The next time I woke up it was the next morning. Through a fog, a police officer came and interviewed me and asked me did I see who hit me, and I told him no.

"I don't know what happened. Someone hit me out of nowhere."

After that, I kept dozing in and out. There were two other beds but no patients.

I opened my eyes and a Dr. McCrutcheon was standing at my bedside. "Doctor, I'm pregnant," I blurted out. "I hope my baby is okay."

"Yes, your cervix is intact. Your baby is fine. We're going to keep you another night for observation though."

"Are you sure about the baby?" I heard myself saying. I rubbed my stomach in a circular motion. For the first time I felt protective of my unborn child. *Oh, Lord, don't let anything be wrong with my baby.*

"Yes." The doctor paused, absently shaking his head, as if in disbelief. "You're both a living miracle. It looks like your baby will be fine, but I'd like you to stay on bed rest for the next week or two. We'll keep you one more night to be sure, then release you tomorrow morning. Make sure you see your doctor next week. "

A tall, lithe Jamaican nurse, whose badge read Eurie Harris, RN, pushed in a heart monitor machine for the baby. She took out a magic wand and put it on my stomach, which was still flat. I heard this "slosh, slosh, sloshing" sound, which resembled the noise a washing machine makes. A strong rhythmic pony trot filled the room.

"That's your baby," the nurse said in her lilting Jamaican accent. My baby's heartbeat sounded like the most beautiful symphony ever written.

"You're not bleeding either," she continued. "Your cervix is closed. The baby seems fine."

She pointed to a flashing point on the screen. "That's your baby's heart. Here's the head. The body."

"Can you tell the sex of the baby?"

"Not yet. At twenty weeks. You're almost twelve weeks. Here, I can give you a picture though."

I gazed down at the ultrasound picture in amazement. For a moment, I caught my breath. I'd never seen anything more beautiful—this tadpole-looking piece of protoplasm in this cloudy, dark photo. Then I just broke down, tears oozing down my face. My baby was alive—the baby I almost aborted.

Maybe this was a miracle. We both could have been killed. I could have lived but lost the baby, but neither situation happened. For the first time I felt a butterfly-feeling flutter in my stomach. In awe, I reached down and gently touched my stomach, which was still as flat as an ironing board. Feathers trembled in my stomach again. What was that? Then it hit me. My baby was moving!

Suddenly I didn't care who the father was. This was my baby. He or she had a right to live. My mother, Venita, gave birth to my brother at age fourteen and to me at sixteen, and she survived. Besides, how old did I have to be to have a baby? Who's to say I'd ever get pregnant again? I was now thirty-five. I thought about what Chica told me about her abortion and how it left her sterile.

"Thank you, Lord," I silently prayed, grateful I didn't get the abortion. I made a silent vow to my unborn child: *Well, it's me and you. I'll try to keep you safe and be a good mother. I don't know how, but I'll learn how.*

I reached in my purse and found my iPhone. I called my foster mother, Shirley, and told her about my car accident.

"Are you all right?"

I could hear the concern in her voice. I was surprised though, since she was still caretaking my foster father, Daddy Chill, who had dementia. Shirley always seemed more overwhelmed than I ever remember her being when we were growing up. But recently, she put him in an adult daycare center where she got a little relief for six hours each day. She really sounded like she heard me for the first time in a long time.

I thought about how this was my second time I almost died, the first time being when I was shot on the LAPD. Somehow this near-death experience made life even more precious; especially now that I had my unborn child's life to consider. "Yes, I'm fine. The doctor said I'm a walking miracle, but there's something I want to tell you."

"What is it?"

I paused. *Should I tell her?* Something egged me on. "I'm pregnant." It was as if putting my condition into words made it real. Announced it to the universe. I was going to be a mother! Now that I'd said it, this pregnancy felt real.

"What?" Shirley shrieked. "I knew it. I knew something was different about you. Oh, my God. Are you and the baby all right?"

"Surprisingly, we're fine. I'm scared, though."

"Don't worry. The Lord never gives you more than you can handle."

"I don't know."

"Well, at least you will have a piece of Romero. I know how much you loved him. Life is strange like that. God taketh away and He giveth."

I hesitated. I couldn't tell Shirley I wasn't sure about the paternity. She was the second person, the other being Chica, who had said I'd have a piece of Romero; I sure hoped so.

"I guess it is."

Next, I got a call from my brother Mayhem, the reason for my dilemma in the first place. I hadn't talked to him since the shootout that freed him from his abductors.

"Hey, Z. I need to see you." He was always blunt and to the point.

My heart beat speeded up. For the first time, I got in touch with what I was feeling toward my brother, a born and bred criminal—pissed off, mad as all get-out, red-hot angry. I blamed him for this mess I was in. I would have never been in this dilemma in the first place if it weren't for his kidnapping. Why did he have to come to me and get me involved? Now I'd truly walked on the wild side. I didn't really know myself anymore.

Yet, even so, I was angrier at the two men who set up his kidnapping. I promised I was going to make someone pay for this. *This isn't over yet.*

"I'm in USC."

"What happened?"

"Minor car accident. It looks like I'll live though."

"Cool. I'll be right over to see you." He hung up without saying good-bye.

A dark sense of foreboding hit me. Mayhem and the word "trouble" were synonymous. What did he want now? You have to know something about Mayhem. He was a second-generation Crip, (including my mother, Venita, and his biological father, Big Dave, who was a life-long heroin addict). Mayhem was also a kingpin who, ironically, had never used any drugs—even marijuana.

We just reunited a couple of years ago and he'd been nothing but trouble. But what else could I do when he was kidnapped and needed my help to free him? He saved my life when he was a child himself and he saved my life again three months ago, when I was in a shootout, oddly, trying to free him from his kidnappers.

I'd found out my brother had a lot of money—it's just he earned it on the wrong side of the law.

To paraphrase Chris Rock's words from his stand up, *Never Scared*, if you were Black, and earned a lot of money, it had better be on the right side of the law.

What irked me was the fact only Wall Street and banks could sink a world-wide economy into the toilet, and no one go to jail for white collar crime. But do some "black collar crime," and you better believe the judge was going to hand out more time to you, as a Black person, than to your white counterpart(ner) in crime.

Apparently Mayhem didn't think this law applied to him; heshook up the powers that be, and they set up his kidnapping by a Mexican cartel.

My brother wasn't born a Kennedy. Born in Crip territory, South Los Angeles, he was slotted with two spots waiting for him—the penitentiary or the grave. He'd somehow managed to avoid the latter. The Kennedys made their money with bootlegging money, then the parents bought prestige and power, and decided what laws made the powerless the new criminal.

Similarly, my brother made his money from the streets and, from what I'd learned, more recently had made some lucrative investments on Wall Street, pornography Web sites, massage parlors, rap groups, and other legitimate businesses. The American way, wasn't it? Take the land from the Native Americans, bring the Africans over to work it, then become the greatest country in the world at one time. The ends justify the means.

But when a Black man got his money on the wrong side of the law, it was a different story.

Those two fake FBI and DEA agents were going to pay. I didn't know if they were responsible for the bullet that took out Romero; there were so many bullets flying at that fatal shootout. Now, they were, or someone else was, trying to blackmail me over the head I disposed of. But with the pregnancy, I had a new mission.

Right now, my main goal was to have this baby, no matter what came. I decided I could live off my payments from the reality show, and my savings, so I wouldn't have to take too many cases right now.

I definitely didn't want to take on any more dangerous cases—that was, for the time being. All I wanted was a quiet, peaceful pregnancy.

Chapter Six

I must have dozed off because I looked up and there stood my brother, David, aka Mayhem, aka Big Homie, Crip Kingpin, major entrepreneur, dubbed by the DEA agent as "The Steve Jobs of the streets." Mayhem had an imposing posture that reminded me of Suge Knight when he was in his heyday. He kept both of his huge hands folded in front of him, his head thrown back in a regal manner, as if he ruled the world. In a sense, he did rule his world. When Big Homie spoke, people listened. When he said, "Jump," they said, "How high?" He'd been a natural leader all of his life.

His new bodyguard, another big, buff brother, stood on guard in the hallway just outside the door. Mayhem nodded to his guard, then turned his attention to the news.

A flat-screen TV on the wall was blasting, "Bank robbers took police on a four-hour chase from Lancaster through Pasadena to Los Angeles. They wound up in South Los Angeles and began throwing the stolen money out of the car. Onlookers began to pick up money and were obstructing the pursuit. Another car accident in an SUV caused further delay in arresting the suspects. Three were arrested, but one suspect got away."

"Sis, ain't this a bitch? These niggas like Robin Hood. Steal from the rich and give to the hood. Now that's what I'm talking about!" Mayhem struck his right fist in his left palm in approval of the bank robbers' daring attempt at getting away. "The system screws us, and I guess they just wanted to screw the system."

Flabbergasted, I put my hand to my heart while I kept my eyes glued to the TV. "Oh, my God! That must have been what was happening when I was driving up . . . Hey. There's my car." I pointed at the screen. I saw a replay of how the garbage truck hit the robbers' car. It turned my stomach when I saw a picture of my hit-and-run crushed rental SUV being towed by a truck and how pitiful it looked on the TV set. *Dang! How did I even get out of there alive?*

Mayhem got up and walked stealthily around the room. He took a dark handkerchief out of his pocket and covered the surveillance camera they had on the wall. He lowered his voice in a conspiratorial tone. "Sis, I know we haven't talked but I want to thank you."

"Hey, you're my brother. What else was I going to do?"

"Why did you only take twenty thousand dollars out of the account? You know you could have taken more."

"That's my traveling and finder's fee."

"Girl, you could be set for life. I didn't care what you took. I've got other accounts. As long as I have life, I could make some mo' money. How can I ever repay you?"

"All money ain't good money." I caught myself. I didn't want to sound judgmental, but I'd always made my money on what I considered the right side of the law.

Mayhem disregarded my stance. "You still have access to that money if you need it. Here's the new account number on this flash drive so . . ." He handed me a flash drive. "Baby girl, I owe you. You know you the best. Not only did you get that money back from Rio, you saved my life. Girl, you the bomb. How can I thank you?"

Inside, I was thinking, *You've got to be kidding. You don't have any idea what I went through. You can thank me by not asking me to do nothing else for you.*

Mayhem hesitated. "I'm sorry for what happened to your man."

I bit my bottom lip and fought back my tears. There was nothing I could say. I changed the subject. "Do you have any idea about the DEA and this so-called FBI agent who came to me?" I asked. This had been on my mind for some time.

I continued. "Something felt off-kilter about the whole thing. I've been in such a daze, I'm even wondering if they were real. Their names were Agent Richard Braggs and Agent Jerry Stamper. They're the ones who came to me. One had a glass eye."

"I know those fools. Yes, they are real. Greedy bastards. They knew through my record that I was papered down. Those two dirty feds have been paid, but don't worry. I got something for they ass."

Blood pounded in my head. I didn't say anything at first. Finally I spoke. "They claimed you owed them five million dollars. I don't know what I went on that wild goose chase for if you already had the money."

"I had to get my woman back, too. It wasn't just about the money."

"But why would they get involved in a drug deal?"

"Look, people are broke so they will do desperate things. I think they homes was in foreclosure."

I thought of Haviland and her blackmailer who had her over the barrel over faking a home invasion to keep from losing her Hollywood Hills mini-mansion in the height of the recession in 2009. "Do you know if these men are still with the FBI and the DEA?"

"Yes, they still with the DEA and the FBI, with they crooked ass. They shake down more drug dealers than the dealers. I guess when their money got low, they went after me and the money they knew I had from the files on me. They think they untouchable. Plan to retire drinkin' mai tais on some island. Got kids in Ivy League colleges."

"Well, they didn't get the money from me."

"Don't worry. I paid those mothertruckers. They're trying to drain all my money, but that's all right. When I find them, they'll be taken care of."

My heart clutched. "How did you get kidnapped? I've been so out of it, I haven't had a chance to see what was going on. What do they have on you? Why did they set up the kidnapping?"

"Money. Simple as that. I got something on them and they couldn't shake me down anymore.

They figured if they had me abducted they could get a lump sum of money. If it wasn't for you, I would have been killed."

"Another question: did they give you money to go to Brazil?"

"No, they didn't. They found out about the deal and was trying to intercept it and get the money. The cartels wound up keeping Appolonia. That's what I'm here about."

I was hoping to divert him from that subject. "So how did you become a billionaire?"

Mayhem became quiet, as if he was weighing what I'd asked him. He rubbed his clean chin with his right thumb and forefinger. It took what seemed like forever for him to answer. "Good investments on Wall Street."

"Do you think you'll ever get out the game?"

He gave me a strange look. "You know what my philosophy of life is?"

"Shoot."

"I didn't choose my destiny. My destiny chose me. I live in one of the richest cities of America and I just want my part of the California dream. Fuck being broke. Before I get trampled on and never have any power or money, I'll die first. I used to be called an inland terrorist when I was banging, but now I'm trying to go legit. I'm a businessman. It's the American way. You either get, or you get got. We never got money when we were marching for freedom, and now we have no power."

"How about President Obama?"

"Pssssssh." He let out a long hiss. "That was just a fluke. The average Negro ain't living his life."

"I'd—"

"You'd do what if you were in my shoes, born where we were born, and you were a Black man?"

I pondered his question. I lay back on my bed, speechless. I really didn't know what I'd do. "I don't know," I admitted.

"I was trying to . . . I'm just trying to go legit, but that last bid kind of cut into my bank account. Plus, this system won't let a nigga catch a break."

"Not from what I saw in your account . . ."

Mayhem ignored my remark. "Well, anyhow, when I sent Appolonia to Rio that was going to be the last run in that line of business, because there's too much shit going on in Mexico right now." Mayhem pulled up the chair that sat in the corner of the room. "But that's not what I'm here about. I have some questions for you now."

"Shoot."

"What do you know about Tank?" Mayhem leaned close to me.

An image of Tank, beheaded with glazed eyes, flashed like a hologram in my brain, but I shook my head to clear this horrific image. He took that as a "Nothing."

"Well, can you try to find out what happened to Tank?"

"I'll look into it." I felt funny lying to my brother, but I didn't know the whole story. How could I tell him his friend, Tank, his lieutenant, was dead? That he'd been beheaded? "When was the last time he was seen?"

"It was just before you left for Brazil."

For a moment, I remained silent, which was my way of lying. The old me would have been afraid of Mayhem, but after what I saw in Brazil, after what I went through, I was no longer afraid of too much of anything. "I don't know anything."

Tank had been Mayhem's lieutenant, his main man and his muscle. I hated to have to tell him the truth. Tank had been dead for the past three months. I decided this wasn't the time to divulge this information. I needed to find out who was trying to blackmail me first.

"The last time I saw him was when you sent me to get information on how and where to pick up your kids and get them out of L.A. Why?" Now that was a partial truth. That was the last time I saw him alive.

"It seems like you might have been one of the last persons to see him. He's been MIA since about that time."

My heart plunged. I thought when I put in the 911 call from the phone booth about Tank's head, someone would have come and gotten that part of his remains. Obviously not. What happened to his head then? Moreover, what happened to his corpse? Then, who was it who was texting me? Well, who could be trying to blackmail me?

What a mess! I went against what I thought was right in order to help my brother. I mean I got involved with crooked feds/gangbangers/ drug dealers/cartels/strippers/porn stars, in the quest to free my brother. Yes, I helped get him away from his kidnappers, but at what cost? I lost my man, I lost my integrity, I'd added more sins on my list, and now I was trying to cover up my lie.

Who saw me dump Tank's head, which was inside the basket? Was it Agent Braggs? Was it Agent Stamper? Now I had lied to my brother, saying I didn't know where Tank was. Was this how you crossed the line? With one lie, then another?

I changed the subject. "Have you heard from Venita?" I wasn't sure which city my mother had fled to with her three grandsons, Mayhem's "little thuglets."

"Yes, she's safe with the boys. I've already told her to come on back. They will be safe now. But they gon' have to stay with Venita for now. After I go get their mama, the boys can come back home." He let out a deep sigh.

"Z, I'm going to need you to go back to Brazil. Look, we gon' have to go put some work in."

So that had been his agenda all along.

"What?" He might as well have punched me in my solar plexus. "Run that by me again." I pursed my lips like "Really?"

"I'm going to Brazil to get Appolonia. I'd like you to go with me since you know the territory."

"Hold up! What did you say?" I paused for dramatic effect and emphasis.

"Aw come on, sis. I've got to get Appolonia back. I'd like to get my kids back and they're going to need their mom to take care of them while I work."

I held my hands up in surrender. My eyes dive-bombed into his, and the person who most people were afraid to look into the eye saw a fool equally as crazy on the other end. "I know you've lost your freakin' mind."

At first, David, who was used to giving orders, looked shocked to see me not comply, and a furrow of anger crossed his brow, but then he settled into a look of amusement.

"Well, now I know you my sister for sure. You know you got fire in you, girl."

I hesitated, and picked my words carefully.

"Listen, Mayhem. You my brother, and I've put in work for you, but, baby, the price was too high. Besides, David, there's a lot you don't know about Appolonia." How could I tell him that she had been in a witness protection program for the past fifteen years and that her real name was Samaria? That she had a teenager daughter by a drug lord who had gotten out of prison and set up the drug deal in order to get her back?

"Look, I know she has a past, but who doesn't?"

I don't know where my boldness came from but now I do know this: I'd invested a part of my life in Mayhem's life, which had changed my whole destiny because of his mess, and I had a right to be bold and speak my mind. I started to divulge what I knew, but something held me back. I couldn't tell him that Appolonia was a willing prisoner. Diablo was her oldest child's father, the child she gave birth to at fourteen, just before she turned state's evidence on Diablo and went into protective custody.

After a long silence, Mayhem started to try to break me down. His head rubbernecked as he mean mugged me. "Why won't you help me?"

"Why should I? Besides, what so special about her? You can have any of these women out here. How about that one at your club?" I snapped my finger. "What was her name? Cinnamon or some type of spice?"

"Who? Chutney? I don't care about her. Look. I can't help who I love."

"Let's get one thing straight. I'm not going to go back to Rio. But I'll tell you what I learned: it's dangerous. In fact, it's suicide."

"So you won't go with me?"

"I can't."

"Why not?"

"I'm pregnant. I . . ." There. I'd said it for a second time to a family member.

Mayhem's face shifted from the hard lines to a softness I seldom saw in him as he interrupted me. "Are you happy? Is it for dude who got killed?"

I hesitated. How could I tell him I wasn't sure? "Yes." My voice came out barely above a whisper.

"He was a stand-up dude. You know I think your man saved my life. He found out I was your brother and he told his fam to hold off until you got back with the money."

"What?"

"No shit. Your man did that for me."

"Well, how can you go out the country anyhow? Aren't you on parole? Don't you have a parole officer?"

"I can handle that. I got an insurance policy where I can come and go in and out the country when I get ready. But on the real, I've got something I want you to put in a safe place for me."

I looked down at another flash drive.

"This is my passport out the country and back without violating my parole. This is for you, too, if you need any money. The password is on the flash drive with the account number. It's out of the Cayman Islands. If I get detained, I trust you to get money to my lawyer. Here's his name and number." He handed me a business card to an Attorney Donald Solomon, which I later put into my phone.

I read the subtext here. *Uh-oh.* A frisson went through my bone marrow. I had this strange feeling. Déjà vu. My gut went to churning. I went through this with Okamoto, my former, now deceased police partner, on the night he was murdered. He'd given me a key to his safe deposit, which had information in it which almost cost me my life.

But something else was on my mind, eating at me.

"Did you turn state's evidence? Are you a snitch?" Now that I'd shaped the words, they felt scary, like Mayhem might kill me for saying it, but it was necessary.

Now it was his turn to get quiet, like, "Are you crazy?" His face contorted in anger. "Hell naw," he said. "Just say I got a list. I know dirt on people all the way to the top. I have information on a secret society that runs this country. These white men will make the Ku Klux Klan seem like choir boys. I know about judges who've been paid bribes to fix cases. I'm a good guy when I see some of the things these politicians have done.

"I want you to be able to get into my safe deposit box downtown at Bank of America. Here's the key for you, too, if anything happens to me. I want you to get this information to the FBI. My lawyer will know who the good guys are." Mayhem looked away.

Unlike what happened with Okamoto, this time the stakes were higher. He was talking about a secret society.

My mind was diverted to something else that was bothering me. "Why do you want to go to Brazil to take crack? I heard they were cleaning up the drugs in Rio for the 2016 Olympics."

"I don't want to go there to do business this time. This is personal."

"You mean for Appolonia? You don't even know her."

"How did you feel about dude?"

"Romero?"

"Yeah."

"I loved him. I would've taken a bullet for him. I feel awful that he died because he got involved for me."

"Well, he gave his life for you. That's how strong his love was, and I only knew of him. . . . Now that was some love. This is what I've got to do. I can't just throw wifey under the bus."

"What do you mean?"

"I'm the reason Appolonia went back to Rio in the first place. I think she's being held against her will."

"Maybe you need to leave that alone. Plus, it's dangerous to go to Rio right now."

"You never told me what happened in Brazil."

I shook my head. Some things were too painful to remember, let alone talk about. I didn't want to tell him that she was back with Diablo, who was now his archenemy and his rival.

Finally, I spoke up. "Bro, let's just say your sister's life will never be the same behind that trip."

Mayhem stared at me and I could tell he knew that it had been a trip to hell and back. "I'm sorry, sis." He reached out and hugged me.

"Sometimes I could choke your neck just for getting me involved."

Mayhem chuckled. I could hear my brother's baritone voice vibrate in his large chest through his laughter. I noticed he had a nice laugh. He was not a person who laughed often. He always looked "hard."

"Now, I know you my sister. You did it because I was your brother."

"Speaking of family, you know I heard from our baby sister, Righteousness—at least she's claiming to be her. She says she has her birth certificate. She was adopted and is living in Michigan."

"Does she know where our baby brother, Diggity, is?"

"I don't know. We were supposed to talk when I got home, and now I'm in the hospital. I'm really too shook up to call her right now. I'll call her when I get home. But as for Diggity, I think they were separated when she was adopted."

"Say what? Well, if anyone can find him, it will be you. I have faith in you, sis. You the bomb when it comes to finding people."

"Whatever." I flagged my hand in a dismissive way. "Anyhow, I was on my way home to talk to her when there was something going on crazy in South L.A. Money was floating down in the street. I didn't know if I was hallucinating at the time, but now I see what was happening on the news."

"Yeah, I heard about it on the way here too. So that was where you were in the car accident? Girl, you know you always be in some heat. "

I once considered my brother a killer and now I was a killer too. Even if my killings were in self-defense, how could I judge? I'd still taken six lives. I didn't even want to think about it.

I'd been angry with God and, in turn, with Mayhem since Romero's death. I blamed God for letting it happen, and Mayhem for getting me involved. But now I knew I had to take some responsibility for what happened. I had a choice. I could've not gotten involved.

Well, one thing for sure. I wouldn't get involved in Mayhem's mess this time around.

Chapter Seven

The next morning, I caught a cab home from the hospital, thinking about this new turn of events. I thought about how capricious life could be. One minute you're okay and, the next, you're hit by a car. Life could change on a dime. I could have died, I could have lost the baby, but I didn't die and I didn't miscarry. Miraculously, we were both alive and safe. Wasn't that a sign from God that this baby was meant to be? For the moment, I felt like everything would work out fine.

Before my discharge from the hospital, I had spent the morning on the phone, contacting the rental agency to pick up the car from the police station's impound. (The insurance would cover everything.) For a moment, my mind was off whoever was threatening to turn me in for disposing of Tank's head.

Now, I was beginning to feel a surge of excitement over the baby. I had to say the words out loud because sometimes I couldn't believe it. I was actually going to have a baby. I was going to be a mother! And I was alive! I was really happy to be alive! Even the fronds on the palm trees stood at attention, as if they were bending down to welcome me home as I rode up the hill to the tri-level located in Baldwin Hills, one of the best-kept Black neighborhoods in L.A. Overcast, slate grey sky, yet I was in a good mood. Yes, life was good.

I didn't stop in "the big house" to see my foster mother, Shirley, foster father, Daddy Chill, or my nieces, Chica's daughters, Soledad, Malibu, Charisma, or Brooklyn. I just clambered upstairs, to my bachelor garage apartment, spread a clean sheet on my futon, climbed on it, pulled up my warm afghan cover, and passed out.

I don't know how much time passed, but I woke up to the sound of rain, sleet, and hail beating a double-dutch rhythm on the roof. The sound of a loud thunderclap made me jump. I could see lightning flashing through my skylight window.

I lay there in a languid mood, remembering the first time I slept in Romero's arms on this futon. We didn't have sex on that first date—instead, we talked all night; then he just held me while I dozed off. Since his death three months ago, I'd spent more time in my garage apartment than I'd spent there in the past year. I'd generally stayed over at Romero's house in Silver Lake when he was alive. I guessed I'd have to think about moving, now that I'd have a baby to care for. Plus, this apartment had a lot of bad memories.

I'd been so upset while I was in mourning, I had forgotten about the two crooked undercover cops, Flag and Anderson, who I'd killed in this very same apartment. True, it was self-defense, but now I felt a little uncomfortable being in the same space I murdered two men in. Maybe it was the pregnancy that made me see everything in an ultra-sensitive light. One thing was for sure, I would need a larger place when I had the baby, but I'd have to worry about that later.

Like a schizoid person, I went from feeling happy before I lay down to feeling melancholic when I woke up. Being the movie buff I am, I thought a movie would perk me up and decided to play a DVD from my collection: *The Howlin' Wolf Story—The Secret History of Rock & Roll*, a documentary on the life of this iconic guitarist, blues singer, and harmonica player, Howlin' Wolf, aka Chester Arthur Burnett. *Now what did I do that for?* When the blues song "Smoke Stack Lightning" played, I felt as if I was on one of those old-fashioned trains, and I experienced

the haunting longing in the music in each turn of
the wheel. I missed Romero so, I could feel him in
each blues note. I cut the DVD off.

Next, I watched some of my old video tapes of
Alex Haley's *Roots*—where Kizzy, Kunta Kinte's
daughter, cried about how everyone she had
loved, including her mother and father and her
first love, had been taken from her. She was sold
away from her parents and her first love was
sold away when their aborted plot to escape was
discovered.

That was all it took. The dams really broke and
I boohooed over the loss of Romero. I cried over
my mother, Venita—whom I still hadn't forgiven
and who had abandoned me when she went to
jail when I was nine years old. I wept over the
loss of my late Belizean father, Buddy, who was
murdered. Also I sobbed for the loss of my three
siblings when we were all shipped to different
foster homes. My only biological sister had been
lost to me for all these years, and I hoped this
Rachel was really our baby sister, Ry-chee, the
nickname we used to call Righteousness. I only
had Mayhem left. Life was so unfair.

"Show me a sign you're still here," I said out
loud to the room, talking to Romero as I wiped
my eyes. My murdered father still came to me
in my dreams. I'd been speaking to Romeo a lot
since his death, but I couldn't feel his presence.

Suddenly, I felt a furry ball flash by my feet; I looked down to see Ben, my pet ferret, nestled at my feet and I felt a sense of comfort. I took solace in the fact I still had my pet and had kept him alive for a couple of years, which was part of my treatment plan from my alcohol rehab program. Absently, I fluffed his mousy grey fur.

Something prompted me to pick up my phone to see if there were any messages from my sister, Rachel. There were none from her. Bummer.

I really hadn't listened to my voice messages on my iPhone since I came from Brazil. Following Romero's death, I'd been so depressed I had only answered a few direct calls. If they wanted to talk to or see me at all, Chica and Haviland would just come and drag me out the house. That's how they were able to get me to the set to help shoot shows, even if I moved around like a zombie. That's how we were able to shoot the pilot and the first set of shows for our reality show.

Besides being depressed, I had been so busy shooting our reality show, for the first time since I had bought the new phone with the same number I had before I went to Brazil, I checked my message center. I had only called out to clients, or answered a few calls from Chica and Haviland.

The first frantic call on my voice mail came from Chica on the previous day. "Where are you, Z?" I clicked delete. I'd talk to Chica later.

I clicked my next message. A familiar voice came on the line. My heart almost stopped. I couldn't believe what I was hearing! It was a message from Romero. My first thought was, *maybe they made a mistake.* Maybe he wasn't dead. Then I saw the image of him dying in my arms. So I listened again to the message. I saved the message, then went back through the center. This voice mail was dated back to three months ago while I was still in Brazil. It almost scared me because it was like hearing his voice from the grave. His voice reminded me how thin the line was between life and death. One minute you were here, and the next minute, you're on the other side of life.

"Z, this is Romero. I want you to know I love you. I found out about your brother's kidnapping. He's safe—for now . . . ."

A long pause ensued. His voice sounded tired. "I hope you're okay. Oh, baby, why didn't you tell me? Anyhow . . . what I want you to do is contact my lawyer, Attorney Jay Stein, in Pasadena. His phone number is 1-818-693-8888. Call him just in case anything happens to me. Love you, *mamacita.* Hope to see you soon."

My heart clutched, then began to fibrillate. Tears gushing down my face, I listened to the message over and over. I knew it was sick to do this, but I savored every word. If only I could touch him and see him again.

Finally, I called the attorney, Stein, and scheduled an appointment for the next week.

"I can't come in this week, but I'll come next week." I almost added, "I'm on bed rest." But I caught myself.

That evening I called Rachel as I lay on bed rest. She answered on the first ring. "Hello, may I speak to Rachel?"

"Is this my big sister, Z?" she asked in a timid voice.

"Yes, baby sis," I said, using the nickname I used to use for her when I was young.

She spoke in a rush. "I almost thought you weren't going to call me anymore. That you might have thought this was a prank."

"Oh, no, baby. I'm so sorry I didn't call you. I've been in a car accident since we spoke. I just got out the hospital today."

"Are you all right?"

"Yes, I'm fine. You know I've been looking for you for the past three years. I've dreamed about this day for years."

"Me too."

"What are your adoptive parents like?"

"They're good. Both are retired school teachers. They put me through college and grad school."

"But, tell me about you."

"Well, I'm engaged, I'm twenty-six, and I'm a kindergarten teacher. I wanted to know something about my family before I get married and have children."

Babies . . . Some women actually want children? Well, now I'm going to be a mother, ready or not. Here I come. "Are you happy?"

"I'm happier now that I can get to know my roots. You don't know how long I've wanted to find you."

"Same here. Do you know where Diggity is?" Diggity, my baby brother, whose real name was Daniel, was a year older than Rachel. They were living in separate foster homes the last time I saw them.

"I don't know. He was adopted by another family around the same time I was when we were nine and ten and I lost touch with him. I've always wanted to meet my mom. How is she?"

"She's all right. She's out of town right now, but she should be back soon. Just say our family is a little dysfunctional."

"I do realize that. After all, I was born in a prison. I have two birth certificates: the one from my real mother, and the amended one when my adoptive parents adopted me. . . . But you seem to be doing well, in spite of everything."

"I don't know about all that now."

"Oh, you're being modest."

"Why do you say that?"

"I Googled you."

"This Internet is a mess. What did you find out?"

"I see that you're a private eye and you have a reality TV show called *Women in Business*."

I didn't answer. These two titles were my masks. If she only knew the real Z: the one who was about to abort her baby up until this car accident made me realize I wanted my child; the one who killed four men in Brazil, trying to save my brother.

I can't remember everything we talked about but we talked almost two hours. No matter how long we talked, you could never catch up a lifetime in that time.

As soon as I hung up, I called my birth mother, Venita, on her latest phone card throwaway cell phone and told her the good news—that I'd found Ry-chee.

"For real? Are you serious?" She started screaming like a wild woman; then she burst out into loud sobs, almost piercing my eardrums.

"I heard you'll be back in town soon," I said after Venita calmed down.

"I'm supposed to come back in a couple of weeks, after I wrap up my business here. I've got a job I'm going to give notice to. The boys are in school through the mosque, but they'll be out for summer vacation."

"What?"

"Yes, these boys just needed some discipline. We've been studying with the Nation of Islam since we came to Chicago. At first we stayed in Iowa until Mayhem was freed. Thank you so much, Z."

"Well, he *is* my brother . . ."

"Anyhow, I've been taking the boys to the mosque so they are learning about their history and how to be good Black men."

"My, my. Aren't you full of surprises?"

"Well, life is about change. For the first time, I'm feeling whole." Venita paused. "I haven't felt right since I gave birth to Righteousness in prison. I promised myself that one day I would see her again. That's when I hit rock bottom and made a vow to God that I would change. But, what about Diggity?"

Venita was referring to my youngest brother, Daniel, whom we'd nicknamed Diggity because, when he was in his diaper, he used to break down and work it when he danced until Venita would say, "Hot diggity dog. Look at that baby go!" When the song "No Diggity" came out in 1996, I always thought of my baby brother.

"We've still got to find him," I said. "They were adopted by different families."

Venita started crying again. This was disconcerting for me—this new emotional mother. I thought back to how she cried when she saw her grandsons for the first time last year. Ironically, I never saw her shed a tear when we were growing up; and she had plenty to weep about while she was gangbanging and fighting with her men.

I guessed I felt sorry for her. "Okay. Well, I'll make sure Ry-chee comes to visit you when you come home."

"Praise Allah!" she shouted between tears.

What? When did she get so religious? I wondered.

Chapter Eight

After I showered, I called Shirley and told her I was home from the hospital and on bed rest.

"How long will you be on bed rest?" she asked. "You need anything?"

"Just for about a week and some change. Can you bring some food? I'm starving. This is the first day I haven't felt nauseated in months."

"Sure. I'll cook you up some turnip greens and chicken soup. I'll make you some Jell-O, too. That should help settle your stomach. Try some crackers."

"Yummy." For the first time in three months, I had an appetite and felt like eating.

"I remember my first pregnancy. When I finally got over the morning sickness, I was ravenous."

Later that evening, Shirley came up to my garage apartment, crock pots of cooked food in tow. She'd even made one of my favorites—salmon croquettes.

"You can freeze some and heat them up. This should get you through a few days," she said, putting the food in my small refrigerator.

"Thank you, Moochie." I kissed her cheek when she reached down and hugged me. I decided to tell Shirley the good news. "Guess what?"

"What? You're full of surprises. I hope you're not pregnant with twins."

"No, I don't think so. But it's something just as miraculous."

"What is it? Tell me."

"I found my baby sister, Ry-chee." My voice sounded dry.

"What? Wonderful! Then, why are you looking so down?"

"I don't know if I did the right thing. I told Venita, but now I'm having second thoughts. I don't want to share her with Venita."

Shirley paused for a long time. "Of course, you did the right thing. Your mother has a right to know. That's her child."

"She wasn't any mother to her. She dropped her out and left her in a prison hospital."

"Well, Venita was incarcerated when your sister was born. It wasn't like she had much choice."

"I guess so."

"Look, you have to forgive your mom," Shirley said, giving me a serious look. "She has tried to make amends with you, and you keep rejecting her."

"No, she has made amends with everyone but me. She's taking care of Mayhem's kids right now, albeit on the run with them. She even sucked me in to help free this fool and it has made a mess of my life."

"What mess? Don't you know life is a gift from God? Remember how I told you I lost my firstborn child and was never able to conceive again?"

"No, I didn't mean that. Don't get me wrong. I'm glad about the baby. I was just a little shook at first."

"Look you need to resolve these issues with your mom. You don't know what you might need your mom for."

"She's not my mom. You're my Moochie." That was the nickname I had for my foster mother, Shirley: the one who got me through my teen years without me having a baby because she guarded my foster sister, Chica, and me like prize pumpkins at a fair. Although Chica got pregnant at eighteen with her deceased son, Trayvon, she'd moved out the house and was on her own when she became a teen mom. Definitely not on Shirley's watch.

Besides, Shirley was the one who sat through my detox withdrawal from alcohol three years ago. No, she was my mother in every sense of the word.

"Child, you don't have to brownnose with me. I know you love me and I love you too. But Venita's your birth mom and I want to see you guys heal and get close to each other. You won't be whole until you forgive her. Forgiveness frees us. When we hate, we keep the carbon copy."

I didn't answer. Anger rose up in my chest and I had to breathe deeply to calm down. "Well, what do you think I should do with Rachel when I meet her?"

"Give her plenty of love."

Later, my foster nieces, Malibu, Soledad, Charisma, and Brooklyn came to see me. "Auntie, are you really having a baby?" Brooklyn, who was now eight, asked.

"That's what the doctor says."

"Wow! We're going to have a baby cousin. Awesome," Malibu, the fourteen-going-on-forty-year-old chirped. She was such an old soul, it scared me sometimes. She was the one who tried to keep the family together when Trayvon, her fifteen-year-old brother, was murdered two years ago, and Shirley lost her mind for a while. Malibu had cooked, taken care of her younger sisters, and even tried to take care of Daddy Chill, who, unbeknownst to us at the time, had dementia. Although she had the body of a twenty-one-year-old, you could look in her face and see the innocence still there.

At last, the family was settling down, and here I was, pregnant with a baby. I guessed, in a way, this was good news after all we'd gone through together as a family; but then I thought about the message I might have been sending as a single woman to young, impressionable girls.

"Now listen, girls. Don't go get any romantic ideas in your heads about having babies without a husband. I'm a grown woman and this is scary without a husband. I was planning on marrying Romero before he died. Don't try to act like that *Teen Mom* show. I want you girls to be married when you start having babies, you hear me?"

"Don't worry," Malibu said, slinging her waist-length wavy hair over her shoulder. "G-Ma has given us the talk. She says boys tell pretty girls and ugly girls all the same thing. Sex doesn't have a face. If you have a baby, you won't be able to go to prom and the boys will be off with someone else, laughing at you, while you're stuck with a baby."

"You'll be left holding the bag," we all said in unison. Even Brooklyn knew the "talk." I laughed at how effective that sex talk had been for Chica and me too.

The girls scrubbed and cleaned my apartment and I felt like a queen. They took Ben in his cage to visit at "the big house."

Chapter Nine

While I was on bed rest over the next week, I watched *Training Day* (my current DVD from Netflix) so many times until I knew most of the lines backward and forward. Watching this film made me think of my days in the Los Angeles Police Department. It often made me wonder about my tenure as a law enforcement officer. Ten long years I gave of my life. Did I regret it? No. It was my destiny. It was what brought me to being a private eye.

Yet one thing I knew for sure was I never questioned if I crossed the line from the good guys to the bad guys back then, even with my alcohol problem. But now I often asked myself: had I crossed the line since I became a PI? I didn't even want to answer that question.

To pass time over the week I was on bed rest, I even began to play chess with myself. I taught myself to crochet and started making a baby blanket. I made some origami flowers. I worked

crossword puzzles. I learned Sudoku. I scheduled an appointment with an ob-gyn doctor, an
African American female, Dr. Gail Henderson. I
ordered and downloaded books on pregnancy,
childbirth, and parenting for my Amazon Kindle,
and started studying up on a doula when I read
an article and found out that one of my favorite
artists, Erykah Badu, delivered babies. I was
already thinking of a home delivery with all my
loved ones to welcome my new baby.

I researched DNA tests during pregnancy,
to see if I could establish the paternity of the
child, but when I saw that there was a risk of
miscarriage, I changed my mind. I would have to
know Romero's blood type, which I didn't know.
I resolved that I would not do the test, and would
wait and see what happened.

I was also able to do research into Agent
Stamper's and Agent Braggs's lives. I was able
to hack into the DEA frame and the FBI frame
to get information on them. Their records were
clean. I Googled them and found they both had
won awards in their jobs. Of course, I couldn't
find anything about a covert operation where
they would have given Mayhem the money to go
to Brazil.

Both were married with three and four children, respectively. They both participated in
bake sales at their children's school. They even

volunteered at the homeless missions in downtown L.A. at Thanksgiving and Christmas. But, my first red flag was that they lived in Bel Air and Beverly Hills, which are expensive areas. They both had children in Ivy League colleges and minor children in private schools. They both drove Lamborghinis, in addition to owning two Cadillac SUVs, and two Rolls-Royces apiece. I looked up the average salary and they both lived beyond that. My gut told me this didn't add up.

I did some more on my search for my brother Diggity aka David de la croix. I had a list of people named David de la Croix who were born in 1985 in California. I felt horrible as I did it, but I checked the death certificates for the past ten years and I checked the prison system. Each time it came back negative, I would let out a sigh of relief.

I decided I wouldn't take any money from Mayhem's account, unless it was for his lawyer. I in no way wanted to get involved in his madness. If I didn't use his money, I wouldn't feel any obligation.

I started trying to figure out a plan to find out what happened to Tank, my brother's lieutenant. I knew his head had been cut off, but where was his body? I did some searching for Tank. I called F-Loc, OG Crip, and my street informant.

"Hey, Loc."

"Where you been, Z?"

"I went out the country. Do you know anything about Tank, who was my brother's lieutenant?"

"Naw, ain't nobody seen him. He been ghost like a mug as far as I know."

"Can you see what you can find out?"

"I'll put word out on the street and see what I can come up with."

"Thanks."

"Sho'nuff. Take care, baby girl."

After I hung up, I wondered, *where could Tank's body be? Did his head got picked up when I put in the 911 call before I flew to Rio?*

Wherever his body was, he needed to be put to rest.

I wondered what happened to my black-mailers. For the moment, I hadn't heard from whoever it was. What would be their next move?

"Two wrongs don't make a right," Shirley said to me when I told her how I almost regretted telling Venita that I'd found Ry-chee. It seemed unfair that she should share in our reunion, but from what I learned from Rachel, she really wanted to see her mom. A real *Leave It to Beaver* family moment. Yuck.

"I don't know. It just doesn't seem right that she should benefit from all my searching. I've gone to the Adoption Central Registry, which didn't come to anything since Ry-chee and Dig-gity never signed up. I've interviewed the foster parents who last had Ry-chee, and the one who last had Diggity. I've begged social services for their records, to no avail. It's the weirdest thing that I found Ry-chee through social media."

"Yes, this social media is something else. But, baby, you've got to let your sister meet your mother. If you didn't and your sister found out later, that could blow up in your face."

I heaved a sigh. "I know, I know," I conceded.

I struggled to beat down my sense of jealousy. I was the one who found Rachel, yet Venita was going to get all the glory. I guessed "mother trumped sister." Just like "wifey trumped sister," when it came to Mayhem.

I guessed who you came out of meant more than who you were related to by sibling-ship. In Mayhem's case, it was like that song, "When a man loves a woman . . . she can do no wrong."

Anyhow, I wanted to get this right this time though. I wanted to make my family whole again. Now underneath I admitted, for the first time, I'd always wanted a family. Now that I was going to have a baby, I wanted a family even more. I couldn't get over it. I—who had never wanted children—was now looking forward to motherhood. I pondered this change in me while I was on bed rest.

Chapter Ten

I decided that with the pregnancy, I would slow down taking cases. I was glad I told Mayhem I would not go to Brazil with him. Who did he think I was? Superwoman? I didn't wear a cape. I'd have to rethink my whole business as a private investigator, now that I was going to be a mother. I'd only deal with safe cases. No more dangerous cases.

No sooner than I thought this, I received a call.

"Hello, are you Zipporah Saldano—the private investigator?"

I had never heard the voice on the other line. "Yes, this is she speaking. Who am I speaking to?"

"My name is Attorney Penny McCord."

"How may I help you?"

"I'm calling against the recommendation of the FBI, and my husband doesn't even know that I'm calling you." I could hear tears in the woman's voice.

"What is the problem?"

The woman took a deep breath. "My husband and I went out of town to a law convention in DC. We left our eighteen-month-old daughter, Kyle, with our nanny, Jill, who is a Nigerian from London. She always seemed to be a responsible person—or I thought she was, but now our baby has come up missing. She claimed that a man in a mask broke into the house, knocked her out, and snatched the baby."

"I'm sorry to hear that. Where is Jill at now?"

"The police had released her, and now we can't find her. We heard you're one of the best in the business. That you can find a needle in a haystack."

"Thank you for your kind words," I murmured.

"I feel so badly now. Jill came highly recommended and we trusted her implicitly with our daughter . . . ." Her voice faltered. "But, I guess we were wrong." She began to weep softly into the phone.

"So how may I help you?"

"I'd like to hire you on the side. The FBI is involved, but they are not moving fast enough for me. I'd like you to help find my baby."

My gut started churning the way it did whenever I sensed something wasn't right. Well, at least this was not a dangerous case; but, then, you never could tell going into a case.

Finally I answered. "I won't be able to meet you for two days, but, in the meantime, I can work the case from my computer."

"You're sure you can't meet me tomorrow?"

"I am really interested in taking your case. You see, I'm going to be a mother too, but I'm under a doctor's care for a couple of more days. I really understand how you must feel. I'd die if anything happened to my baby. I will do searching from my database, but I'll need information from you."

"Thank you, Ms. Soldano. I knew there was a reason I needed to come to you. Congratulations on your baby. How far are you along?"

"I'm about three months." All of a sudden I realized I was becoming a part of that tribe I used to pooh-pooh—the group of mothers who loved to talk about their pregnancies, and their offspring. It felt great, too, even under these dire circumstances, to feel like I belonged to the tribe of women.

"Oh, I remember when I was pregnant with Kyle. I was on bed rest the entire nine months because I'd had four miscarriages, all in the first trimester. I had a surgery that helped me hold her, so as you see, I don't know what I'd do if . . ."

"Look, don't say that. I'll do all I can to help you. With technology, we can track people in ways we couldn't before."

"We've got two good guys from the FBI, but they don't really seem to be sensitive to a woman's feelings."

I took down all the information I could over the phone, and started working on my latest case.

Two days later, after I had my first appointment with Dr. Henderson and I was released from bed rest, I headed to Beverly Hills.

Afterward, I met with Attorney Penny McCord at a restaurant. She was a petite brunette with a pixie haircut and solemn brown eyes. Her eyes were bleary and I could tell she'd been bawling nonstop. She looked to be in her late thirties.

"You can call me Penny," she said after our introductions.

As soon as she sat down, she broke into tears. She was almost hysterical.

"It's gotten worse," she stammered between her sobs. She let me hear a terse message on her iPhone that she'd saved:

"We want $100,000. Do not contact the police or we will kill your little girl. We will cut her up slowly in little pieces."

Just hearing the message, Penny broke down into tears. I patted her back and comforted her, really feeling her pain.

"Let me hear that message again."

I listened one more time. I noted the African-sounding male accent. I had a hunch.

I sat in my car and watched as a SWAT team bum-rushed a room on the first floor at the Marriott Hotel near LAX. I'd given them the tip where the nanny was hiding out. I held my breath and prayed for the toddler's safe return. I still hadn't even cashed the retainer fee check. I didn't know what I would do if anything had happened to this baby. I felt like this case had come to me for a reason.

A half hour later, the place was swarming with FBI agents. About another half hour passed and I looked on as they brought out the nanny and a male, who was later identified as her husband, a Nigerian, who was in the country illegally. They both were in handcuffs.

A female FBI agent came out, carrying the little fat-cheeked baby girl who was chattering away. She was wearing a clean dress with a pinafore, her hair was pulled up in golden-red ringlets, and she appeared to be unharmed.

It was part luck and part skill as to how I tracked little Kyle down. I had asked around at Jill's neighbors' in Westchester about when she was last seen. They said they hadn't seen her, but a man who said he was her husband had been staying at her house recently.

Penny had provided me with Jill's social security number, and I was able to track her down through her debit card. I tracked her last expenses and found her paying for a room at the Marriott.

The first thing I did was call Penny. "Your baby is safe. Go down to Parker Center to pick her up. The missing children's division has your baby."

She broke into tears of joy. "Thank you, Ms. Soldano."

"You're welcome."

"How did you know how to find her?"

"It was just a hunch. I realized when I found out her husband was in the country illegally that he was the one who probably masterminded the entire scheme. I didn't think Jill would hurt the baby, but now she's going down with him."

I thought about how this case made me even more committed to wanting to have my baby. It's like I had discovered a whole new world that I'd never been privy to—the subterranean world of a mother's love.

Chapter Eleven

A week later, as I drove to LAX to pick up my long-lost sister, Rachel, my thoughts were in turmoil. I wanted to get it right this time. I'd always felt guilty, as if I were the reason the family had broken up. I was the one who'd call my father, Buddy, when Rachel's father, Strange, was beating Venita. My father got killed because he was trying to make sure I wasn't molested. My mother went to jail to hide the fact that her then ten-year-old son, Mayhem, had killed her boyfriend, Strange. Through therapy, I'd learned it was not my fault, but I still felt guilty.

I didn't have any pictures of Rachel when she was young. I only had pictures of her in my mind. She was eight going on nine the last time I saw her. She had large buck teeth. She had super thick braids, which she wore behind her ears.

The plane arrived early and I found Rachel waiting in the baggage claim. She had told me she'd be wearing a navy blue jacket. I guessed she

had left the unpredictable weather in Michigan
and didn't realize how warm California could be
at any time of the year.

"Are you my sister?" she said in a baby-sound-
ing voice, which reminded me of the same voice
she had when she was a child.

I nodded. We hugged a little awkwardly.

"Good to see you again," I said.

She looked me up and down, appraising my
black slacks and ankle boots. "I guess I remember you. It's just you look different now."

"I used to wear my hair cut short."

"I remember how you used to bring me gifts
when I was a little girl living in the foster home.
I never forgot you. I was so afraid I'd imagined
you . . . That I'd never see you again." Her eyes
welled with tears.

If I could have frozen this moment in time,
like a butterfly in amber, I would. I thought of
the movie, *Color Purple,* based on Alice Walker's
book, where during all those years, the two
sisters, Celie and Nettie, saw each other through
the prisms of their memories as the same little
girls with "pick tails," and how they felt when
they met. Now I knew why they touched each
other's wrinkles. I cry every time I watch that
ending.

That's how I felt. I fingered Rachel's face. I
held both of her hands in my hands. I glanced

down, looked at her hands, and saw a long lifeline across her right palm, which matched mine. "We both have a long life in front of us."

Rachel blazed this beautiful, even-toothed smile at me when I said that. "I hope we live to be a hundred like the Delaney sisters. Then we can make up for lost time." Rachel's teeth obviously had suffered braces. I was surprised how much she looked like her father, Strange, who was crazy as a Betsy bug, but she also looked like Venita. She seemed to have a sweet personality; totally different from me.

Now she wore her hair shoulder-length in a wrap. Whereas I was a deep café noir color, Rachel was a café au lait hue—like her deceased father, Strange. She was a color in between Venita and me. I wondered, would Venita be color-struck over this light-skinned child she'd given birth to and prefer her to me?

I wanted to get this right this time though. I felt so bad that I caused my little sister to be separated from us as a family. But we were so crazy, I don't know if being with our family would have done her more harm than good.

I was still burbling with excitement, though. It was as if an angel came forth when Rachel contacted me.

I grabbed her weekend roll-on bag and headed to my car in the parking lot across the street from Delta Airlines, wondering what this visit would bring.

Chapter Twelve

I pulled up to the curb of Venita's brick-front, Spanish-style colonial in View Park, an old, established, middle-class Black neighborhood, with its hedges trimmed in silver mist begonias. Her house stood up the hill from Leimert Park and the old Magic Johnson Theater, which was now called the Rave. I was expecting to see the same ghetto fabulous cougar who had left L.A. over three months ago to go into hiding with Mayhem's three sons to keep the Mexican cartels from killing his seed.

Instead, I was in for a surprise. My jaw dropped when I saw my mother. She was wearing an all-white cotton caftan, and donned a head wrap like the Black Muslims. She'd done a 180 since I last saw her wearing a red weave and long fake nails. Her natural nails were now clipped short with a clear polish. She was studying to become a Black Muslim. I guess she even had the boys studying with the Nation of Islam. I noticed the *Final Call* newspaper on the table.

As soon as she saw Rachel, Venita threw her arms around her, kissing her face and sobbing loudly. In fact, they both were in tears. As they stood holding each other, I felt so jealous, I thought I would explode. Finally, Venita pulled away and she hugged me, seemingly as an afterthought. *Strike one,* I thought.

Once we stepped inside the vestibule and across the shining rosewood floors in her living room, Venita waved us into her formal dining room. Mayhem had bought her this old, sixty-year-old refurbished house with the wainscoting, the arched doorways, and the high ceilings. She had beautiful oak molding trimming the perimeter of the ceiling in the dining room. Her sea mist French provincial sofa and loveseat complemented the living room area with her copy of an Emmy Lu masterpiece painting on her crème de menthe walls. Although Venita had only been back in L.A. one week, the floors were shining, and the house was bright and cheery, not dank and dark as if it had been closed up for the three months she was on the run with her three grandsons, Milan, Koran, and Tehran.

"Come on in and eat," she said. She had the table set and waiting. The table was set with white linen, candles, and a centerpiece of hybrid roses that were pink and white, which, I assumed, Venita took out of her yard.

In addition, a bowl of fresh peaches trimmed with strawberries sat on the middle of the table. A crystal bowl filled with lemons balanced the table. She even had a crystal bowl filled with water with a magnolia floating at the top, which gave off a beautiful aroma. Another soft incense wafted on the air and I couldn't quite make out the fragrance, but I thought it was a jasmine scent.

She'd cooked a vegetarian meal of creamy linguine with pan-roasted cauliflower, spinach, and white beans, couscous, chiles rellenos (which used to be one of Romero's favorites), split pea soup, and a green salad. She'd also baked an apple pie, which had the house reeking of cinnamon.

The boys were acting so well behaved I couldn't believe they were the same children I'd met before I went to Rio. Milan, Tehran, and Koran had each grown about two inches over the summer. They no longer wore earrings in their ears and they no longer had the different Mohawks and shag haircuts. They all had their hair cut close to their scalp. I didn't see any more of the "we want to be Crips" personas.

"Hello, Auntie Z," they said in unison. Unlike the little boys who told me I wasn't even their auntie before.

All three came and gave me a hug. They didn't have the same thug bravado they masked when I met them before.

"How did you enjoy Chicago?" I asked Milan, the oldest nephew, who was ten. He seemed to have changed over the summer.

"It was good, ma'am."

My jaw almost dropped to the floor again, but I didn't give away how shocked I was.

Before we ate, Venita led the family in prayer. We held hands and nodded our heads. "Allah, thank you for reuniting my family for me," Venita said. "May you lead us to find my youngest son, Daniel, Zipporah and Rachel's brother.

"I've made a lot of mistakes because I was in darkness and did not know your word and I didn't know my role as the Black woman. I didn't know that I am the descendant of kings and queens in Africa, the offspring of the original woman, Lucy. Please thank you for giving me another chance to be a mother to my adult children and a grandmother to my grandsons. Let me make restitution with my children. May we learn to love one another so we can be a family again. Amen."

With my head bowed, I tried to remember us ever sitting down and eating as a family when I was at home, and I couldn't. We had barbeques with the Crips at a local park, but it was never a family thing. The Crips had been our family back then. I had no nostalgic memories of fond childhood meals, other than cold cereal, hot dogs and beans, and McDonald's, when I still considered it a treat.

For the first time, I felt a piece of some of what had been missing in my life. I guess underneath, we all wanted that Norman Rockwell family tableau.

After dinner we looked at the photo album Rachel had brought with her. It included both of her birth certificates—her original one, and her adoption birth certificate which was created when she was nine years old. I remember at the time how there had been a push to get older Black children out of foster care and into permanent homes. She had brought a lot of photos taken after her adoption, and I showed her some of the pictures I had growing up with Shirley. No one had bothered to take pictures of Rachel when she was in foster care. It was like she'd been invisible. There was a picture taken of her just before her adoption.

"I wish I had more pictures to show you of us when I came to see you," I said wistfully. "But I was so young and foolish, I didn't realize how

important that would have been for you. I was
trying to survive myself. I always had planned
to try to get you once I got on my feet, but after
I got on the police, my schedule was too crazy
to raise children . . . I guess life just got in the
way." I didn't want to add that I became a lush
over those years so I didn't follow-up and visit
anymore.

"That's all right. You were a child yourself."

"I wished I could've done better."

"You're sure you don't have any pictures of you
and Mayhem when you were with our mother?"
Rachel asked in an unbelieving tone.

I shook my head. There was nothing else to
say. Obviously, as a family, we'd never kept a
good photo history. That showed how trifling
Venita had been as a young mother. Thankfully,
both Rachel and I had taken plenty of family
photos with our electronic cameras since we
were adults. Rachel showed me pictures where
she'd gone to Ghana. I hated I didn't have any
pictures of my trip to Rio earlier this year, but
I'd been there on business and had lost my
camera. I hated I hadn't taken pictures of my
nephews when I found them. But we spent the
evening taking pictures on our digital cameras
and making up for lost time.

"I'll start a new photo album," Rachel said.

"Yes, we can exchange our photos through e-mail now," I said.

"Now I've got nephews, a sister, and a mother. When will I meet my oldest brother?"

Venita hesitated. She couldn't explain that she had been on the run with her grandsons because of this infamous oldest son and she herself hadn't seen him lately.

"He's out the country right now," I interjected. "You'll meet him later."

"Okay. Cool beans. I want you all to come to my wedding next year, too."

"For sure," Venita said, smiling.

In her every word and action, I could tell Rachel mourned not being with her mother when she was growing up. One thing was for sure, Rachel didn't know what she'd missed—nothing, as far as I was concerned. Our childhood had been so dysfunctional. I was still traumatized whenever I even thought about it: the weed smoking, the drinking, the uncles who were in and out, the gangbanging, the drive-bys, and the shootings. Please!

Throughout our reunion, I could tell all Rachel wanted was Venita. She wasn't thinking about me, her big sister, who used to struggle to come see her in the foster home even if I had to catch three buses through a series of gang territories

when I was still a teenager myself. But instead
of wanting me, my baby sister's eyes tasted,
licked, and followed Venita's every move. When
Venita chewed, Rachel swallowed. I could tell
she was enamored with our mother. She never
even asked about her father, Strange, who, as far
as the White man's law knew, was murdered by
Venita. I think Rachel knew Venita allegedly had
murdered Strange, but she never brought that
up. I wondered what she would think if she knew
that her half brother had killed her father for
fighting our mother while she was pregnant with
her? I had repressed the memory myself, so no
one knew, besides me, my mother and Mayhem.
Anyhow, Venita took the fall for that murder rap
and did twenty years in prison.

Just from what I was observing, Rachel seemed
as if she had mourned not having her childhood
with my mother. Maybe a child never forgot
being inside their mother's womb, hearing her
voice, rocking to her heartbeat. Maybe there was
always that bond. I didn't know. Unconsciously,
I felt my stomach. Would my baby feel like that
about me? A warm feeling coursed through
me. I would love this baby with all I had, and
hopefully, this baby would love me back.

After dinner, I was surprised when I saw
Venita take Rachel by the hand. "Please forgive

me, baby girl. I'm so sorry I was not there for you. My mind was all messed up with this gang stuff. But now I'm learning how to be a proud Black woman through the Nation of Islam. Farrakhan is the best thing that ever happened to our family. Even the boys are acting better."

She reached over and hugged and kissed Rachel, who melted like a baby in its mother's arms. "I'm sorry I didn't know how to love. I love you so much. I will spend the rest of my life showing you love."

I felt another twinge similar to how I felt when I saw the way Venita reacted to Mayhem's sons after I took my nephews to her to keep the cartels from massacring the three boys. I felt sheer, unadulterated jealousy. Envy of the automatic bond she and the boys seemed to have. Envy for the natural affection Venita had for Rachel. Was it because Rachel was light skinned? Worse, I couldn't stand how my baby sister was just latching on to our mother, Venita. Why couldn't she have been a good mother when I was a child? Why couldn't she have acted like this when we were growing up?

I think what irritated me the most was that Venita was doing the one thing with Rachel that she never did for me. She had never apologized to me for all the crap she'd exposed me to as a child, from causing my father to get murdered in front of my face, to the domestic violence, to being driven in a wild black and white police car without seat belts, then placed in the old, now-defunct McLaren Hall in the middle of the night, which was traumatic in and of itself, on the night my dad was killed and she was arrested.

I could feel the barometer of my repressed rage boiling to a volcanic level, but I tried to calm myself down. *Strike two*.

After we finished taking pictures, Rachel and I washed up the dishes, while the boys went into their rooms to play with their Xbox games. Venita offered to help, but we both said at the same time, "We got this." We laughed, and started feeling a little more like sisters.

Afterwards, Venita, Rachel, and I went into the family room to continue to talk.

Venita turned to Rachel and took her hand. "The worst thing that happened was when you were born and they took you away from me. I'd lost a baby that was stillborn, but to leave a baby in the prison hospital . . . That was one of my lowest points. After that, I started changing while I was in prison.

"Then, earlier this year, Mayhem was kidnapped and I didn't know if I would get him back. But Z helped get my child back safely."

What? Before I knew it, I lost it and went off on Venita. "How can you apologize to her and never apologize to me?" I didn't know where this boldness came from, but I was tired of being the oldest daughter in a Black family—the one the mother leaned on. "And what about Mayhem? He's the reason for all our trouble."

"Haven't I already apologized to you?" Venita's voice sounded uncharacteristically meek, which made me even angrier.

"The truth of the matter is you haven't. It's been a 'too bad, suck it up' attitude toward me. And now that your precious Mayhem has gone back to Brazil, I don't care what happens to him this time."

"Oh, no, you don't mean that, Z. I always hoped you guys would be there for each other when I'm dead and gone."

"Oh, don't guilt me now," I growled.

Venita spoke in a soft voice. "Z, what can I do to make it better between us?"

I got quiet. "You don't get it, do you?" My words were so filled with venom; it surprised me at how much anger I harbored toward Venita. "You're the reason I became an alcoholic, that my life is such a mess now. You were the cause of my father's death. Every time I try to get my life straight, I deal with your life or your son's life, and mine's get messed up."

"Well, I'm sorry you feel this way. David is your brother. Your hating me is not going to bring your father back. I haven't tried to bring trouble into your life, but sometimes we can't outrun our past."

Rachel looked shocked. I guessed she didn't know about all these family secrets.

Venita stood up and came and embraced me. "I love you, Zipporah I Love Saldano." I knew my mother was serious when she called me by my middle name, "I Love."

She continued, "You've become quite a woman and I am proud to be your mother. You're much smarter than I am."

I couldn't answer that. What comeback could you have for that? Rachel came over and hugged and we did a group hug, which made us all cry. My emotions had never felt more raw.

The rest of the evening was rather quiet as we watched old reruns of *The Cosby Show*. I wanted to tell Venita and Rachel that I was pregnant, but something held me back. I wanted to share the ultrasound picture, but I didn't feel this was the right time. Our reunion as mother and daughters was brand new, too fragile.

Rachel and I spent the night at Venita's and, as two sisters, we slept in the same king-sized bed in her guest bedroom. I hated the fact we didn't get to grow up together, but with the age difference, we might have never had the bond Chica and I shared anyway. Chica and I used to whisper across the room to each other from our respective twin beds until Shirley would come into our room and call out, "Go to bed."

The next day, I took Rachel back to the airport by myself since Venita didn't want to say good-bye. Of course, when it was time for her to get off at the airport curb, we both boohooed and kept hugging each other.

I pulled myself together first. I told her, "Let's keep it in the now. We have the present. Let's don't worry about the past."

We promised each other that we would write, e-mail, friend each other on Facebook, call, and stay in touch.

As soon as I left Rachel at the airport for her return flight to Michigan, I drove out of the airport, found a side street, pulled over, put my head on the steering wheel, and cried some more.

Chapter Thirteen

That next week, I think I was still in a state of shock after I left the office of Romero's lawyer, Attorney Stein, in Pasadena. It had been a couple of weeks since I received Romero's posthumous phone message, but, after handling the kidnapping case, I'd elected to see Rachel and Venita first. Now, after visiting the lawyer, I was standing in possession of the deed to Romero's property in Silver Lake and I also had the front door key. I couldn't believe it. I was now the owner of a house that was straight-out paid for. All I would have to pay were the taxes and home owner's insurance.

I couldn't believe my eyes. Romero only asked that I would visit his daughter, Bianca, when possible and establish a relationship with her. When Bianca turned eighteen, he also left money in a trust for his daughter that he wanted me to oversee when Bianca became college aged. I wondered why he didn't leave it for her mother,

Jade, but the divorce had been an acrimonious one.

I stopped at a floral shop, picked up a bouquet of tiger lilies, which used to be Romero's favorite, then headed toward the Inglewood Cemetery, which was Romero's final resting place. I drove through the winding streets of the cemetery and, right away, was struck by the hushed quiet. It was as if the dead didn't want to be disturbed. For a moment, the wail of sirens—which, in Inglewood, was as common a musical backdrop as birds twittering or insects chirping—faded. The silence was eerie. I sucked in my breath and pushed forward. This would be my first time coming to the cemetery since Romero's funeral.

As I made it to Romero's headstone, I noticed a graveside ceremony was in progress not more than forty feet away, but I didn't let it stop me. I placed the bouquet of lilies on Romero's grave, kneeled down, and kissed his headstone. I laid my head on the cool grey slab, and the tears started running down my face. I don't know how long I was leaning up against the headstone.

I talked to Romero so I could still feel close to him. "Romero, thank you so much for leaving me your house. I swear I'll take care of it and keep up the taxes. I will make sure that Bianca is done right by me . . . This was perfect timing—your leaving me the house and all. I really need to move from Shirley's. You know, I'm going to have a baby.

"I hope it's our baby because I don't know if I was raped when I was drugged in Rio. I hope I got pregnant that last night we were together. You were amazing. I'll remember that night as long as I live . . . Then, if anything happened in Rio, I was already pregnant so it would definitely be your baby. I almost had an abortion, but something kept holding me back. Oh, Lord, I hope this is your baby.

"Oh, my goodness. I'm so sorry I didn't marry you, babe. There are so many cases I need to consult with you about. For instance, should I go to the police about what happened to Tank's head, or where is his body? I don't know what to do without incriminating myself, and now I'm being blackmailed.

"Anyhow, I was in a bad car accident coming from Haviland's wedding—yes, Trevor married that fool—I can hear you laughing from your grave." For a moment, I laughed through my tears. "But, anyhow, as bad as this car accident was, I didn't die and I didn't lose the baby. It was like this angel just came forth and held my hand until the emergency crew got there. I wonder what the lady's name was. It reminds me of how you came into my life and kept that gang from raping me when I was eighteen.

"Oh, I miss you so much and I need you."

Suddenly I noticed a shadow fall across the ground in front of where I was kneeling. Startled, I glanced up to see Reverend Edgar.

"Hey, stranger," he said softly.

"Are you following me?" Although he'd startled me, for some reason I really was glad to see him. I wiped the tears in my eyes with the back of my hands. I could tell by the look in his eyes he saw that I had been crying.

"No, I just finished officiating over a funeral, for the son of one of my church members. It was so sad. This young man had just gotten out the gangs and given his life to Christ. Sometimes the streets won't let you go. Everyone is leaving the cemetery now, so I've got a minute." Then he asked me a question. "Your name is Zipporah, right?"

"Yes, how do you know my name?"

"When I took the report, I saw the information on your driver's license. Well, I was wondering, who are you here for?"

"I am here visiting a friend—a former fellow officer. I used to be a police officer."

"Oh, really? Are you still a police officer?"

"No. I'm a private investigator now."

"That's interesting. That's a different profession for a woman. It must take a special type of woman to do it."

"I love it." I assumed he didn't watch our show, and he really sounded as if he didn't know about me, even though the TV cameras were present at Haviland's wedding. "How do you like being a fireman?"

"It can be rewarding. I think I loved the job more when my wife was alive though. Paula was my best friend. I come here often to visit her grave, too. I know how it is to miss someone who meant a lot to you."

I wondered if he had heard some of my conversation with Romero. "How long ago did she die?"

"She died two years ago in childbirth."

"Oh, no! I'm so sorry to hear that." I felt a little afraid, thinking of that. Now I did remember hearing Venita say that when a woman gave birth, she was never so close to death. I said a quick prayer for a safe and healthy delivery. "What happened to the baby?"

A sad look clouded his face. "We had a baby boy. He didn't make it either."

"Oh, my goodness! How did you make it through all that?"

"My faith. God can sustain you through anything. It was hard, but God has held me up and pulled me through. You know the offer still stands for you to come visit my church. After that car accident you were in, you really have a lot to be thankful for."

"You're right about that. I thank—"

Pop. Pop. Pop. Pop. Pop. A round of gunfire blasted in the air, interrupting what I was getting ready to say, which was to thank him for helping cut me out the car when I was in the accident. Birds began to squawk and fly for cover. The remaining mourners in the cemetery scurried and fled to hide behind the parked cars in the circle drive. Fear rippled down my spine.

My heart began to jackhammer and my adrenalin coursed through my veins. *Oh, no!* Was this a gangbanger retaliation shooting at a funeral? They happened all the time. Homeboys showed up for their friend's funeral and ironically would get murdered at the church or the cemetery.

"Get down," I heard Reverend Edgar bellow.

Instinctively, I pushed the reverend, and, from habit, I stopped, dropped, and rolled onto a grassy knoll with a thud. I pulled out my gat, and started firing back in the direction of the shots. I held my stomach with one hand for protection, and shot back with the other. Now how the heck did I get caught in the crosshairs of a shootout? *I thought the gangs had slowed up shooting out at the funerals. Lord, how is this baby going to make it with all this?*

At the same time, I intuitively made sure I fell on my side as I scooted for cover. I noticed that the minister tried to cover my body with his body. But I pushed him to the side as I shot back. The sound of gunfire filled the air.

Fortunately, I'd always been a good shot. The attendees at the funeral were still shouting and running for cover. I made sure I didn't shoot in their direction.

"Oh, Lord, help us!"

"Get Sister Roscoe's walker!"

"Get behind the cars!"

But something in my gut told me that this was no unrelated random shooting.

Finally the cacophony of bullets stopped and I saw someone speed away, burning rubber, in a dark, unmarked car with tinted dark windows.

"Are you all right?" Reverend Edgar asked me, pulling me up from the ground. He brushed the grass off my coat.

"Yes, I'm fine."

"My, you're a good shot. I think you drove our shooters away."

Suddenly I heard my iPhone vibrate. I opened my purse and glanced down. A text message flashed on my screen: We're serious. Next time we'll get you. We will send you instructions.

Now I was wondering if that was a car accident I was in, if that had been intentional, or a random accident. Just in case, I decided I'd move to Romero's house since few people knew where he lived.

"Where is your church?" I asked Reverend Edgar.

"We're on Manchester Boulevard. Here's another card. Fellowship Baptist meets at eleven A.M. on Sunday and we have Bible Study on Wednesday evenings at seven P.M."

Chapter Fourteen

Do not forget to entertain strangers, for by so doing some people have entertained angels without knowing it.

—Hebrews 13:2

That next Sunday I attended Fellowship Church in Inglewood. I was really shaken up by the shootout from the gangs. Something wasn't sitting right in my spirit. The police came out and took a report, but I knew nothing was going to be done. This was just another day in the life of the hood, as far as they were concerned. Fortunately, there were no casualties. Something in my gut let me know things were going to get worse and that there was something going on, but what, I didn't know.

I was beginning to miss church. I had gone to AA meetings, but that connection wasn't enough. Now I really wanted to go to church for the first time in my life. I felt like something was missing in my life.

I also wanted to go to church to thank God for sparing my life and my unborn child's life. I needed spiritual direction as to how to deal with my newfound sister, as well as how to deal with my pregnancy.

As soon as I walked in, I was surprised at how friendly the ushers were and how warm the congregation seemed. The congregation was no larger than about 150 people. People spoke to me in the atrium and were very friendly.

"Welcome," the usher said, handing me a program.

The church was held in a small building. It didn't have the humongous stained-glass windows of the larger mega churches but it truly had the spirit. The choir was rocking the building and making the rafters shake.

As I sat alone, near the back of the church, I wondered, *Lord, can I have redemption for the murders I've committed, even if they were in self-defense?* I thought I'd been thinking about it more since I'd been pregnant. My mind tuned into Reverend Edgar's sermon.

"Sometimes we go through what we feel are unthinkable experiences, tragedies that we think we will never recover from. But I'm here to tell you: with God's help, you can make it."

Reverend Edgar gazed up and saw me sitting in the back of the church, and it seemed like his tone became more dynamic. "I know there are times we feel like Job. Job lost everything. His wife even told him to curse God and die. I know I felt that way when I lost my wife and my newborn son. I said, 'God, why have you abandoned me? How can I go on?' But, I prayed, and through it all, between the help from the brothers and sisters here at Fellowship Baptist, God carried me through. I can't take the credit for coming through this storm.

"I often think of David, the young shepherd boy, and how he went up against the giant. Philistines were giants compared to the average height back then. Their army was mighty. David said in 1 Samuel 17:45 and 46, 'You come before me with a spear, a sword and a javelin, but I am coming to you with the name of Jehovah of armies, the God of the battle lines of Israel whom you have taunted.'

"But David took five smooth stones and was able to go up against the giant and kill him. So we can all go up against the Goliaths of our problems. There is no problem too big that God can't handle."

Awhile later in the sermon, Reverend Edgar said, "If there is anyone in need of prayer, please come to the altar."

I was surprised that I answered the call and
went up to the altar for prayer. Reverend Edgar
looked pleased to see me come up. I didn't join
the church, but I gratefully received the prayers.
After church, as I was leaving, Reverend Edgar
strolled up to me.

"Would you like to go to coffee or tea?"

I started to tell him that I was pregnant and
couldn't drink either beverage right now, but I
changed my mind. "Sure . . ."

Afterward, we drove in our separate cars to the
Starbucks in Inglewood on Century Boulevard.
The place had a nice ambiance, cool jazz flowing
through the sound system, a mixture of cultures
and races typing away on their laptops, or iPads.
I ordered a bottle of water.

"I was happy to see you at church, Zipporah.
I like that name. That was Moses' wife's name."

"Yes, my mother told me that's why she picked
the name." I took a sip of water. I started to
tell him to call me Z, but I decided Zipporah
sounded more dignified. "Thank you for inviting
me. I really enjoyed the service. Yes, my mother
named all of her children out of the Bible."

I often thought of the irony of my mother
naming us out of the Bible when she was a Crip,
but maybe these names had been blessings to us.
Names meant a lot in the hood. They called out

your characteristics. I think our names were so colorful because we were a flamboyant people. Besides, these names made so many of us rise above our circumstances. President Barack Obama. Oprah. Beyoncé.

"Please come back. Don't be no stranger."

"I will."

"I have a question for you," Reverend Edgar said.

"Shoot."

"Do you believe in angels?"

I shrugged. "I'm not sure."

"I don't mean to sound preachy, but I'm a firm believer sometimes angels come into our lives and we don't even know it. Like the scripture says at Hebrews 13:2, 'Do not forget to entertain strangers, for by so doing some people have entertained angels without knowing it.'"

"Well, I know I appreciate you being the one on duty when I was in my car accident. Thank you for staying at the hospital with me until I got stable."

"No problem. That's my job and my Christian duty. I'm not an angel, though."

For a while, a lull fell over our conversation. "Did you remarry since your wife died?"

"No . . . Haven't found the right woman."

"It seems like there are plenty of single women in your congregation."

"That's true. But it would take a special woman to fill Paula's shoes. I haven't felt like that since she died."

"Oh, well, maybe you'll find someone like her."

Reverend Edgar walked me to my car and opened my door. "May I call you sometime, just to talk, to just make sure you're okay?" he asked.

I hesitated. I started to tell him, "Look, I'm pregnant," but something held me back. "Sure."

I checked my back seat to make sure no one was in my car. As I drove home, I kept checking my rearview mirror, to make sure no one was following me. I thought about Reverend Edgar and became curious. I wondered was he trying to hit on me. He seemed interested, but, he was a minister! I couldn't see myself with a minister. No, I decided, he was just being friendly. After all, he did help save my life and cut me out the car.

Later that night, after I got home, I checked my e-mail. I noticed a strange e-mail addy from a government service branch. Not knowing what to expect, I opened it. The e-mail read:

My name is Daniel de la Croix. I think you might be my older sister. I understand you've been looking for me. Although the war is over, I am currently deployed in Iraq. I'm a sergeant. I won't be home for six more months.

"Thank you, Lord!" I said. I wrote him an e-mail back, but I didn't get an answer, but I was still hopeful. *Who knows?* He could have been out on a mission.

I thought about Reverend Edgar's words: "Sometimes angels come into our lives and we don't even know it."

Chapter Fifteen

"Hello," I said, reluctant to make this call.

"Hello, who is this?" The voice sounded hesitant.

I'd only seen Jade, Romero's Black ex-wife, once—when I rode with Romero to take Bianca back home. Often, when he kept Bianca, until the last few months we were together, Romero kept her alone. I was just beginning to meet Bianca, because: one, up until now, I wasn't the motherly type; and two, Romero wasn't the type to introduce his child to women he was dating, unless he felt they were in a serious relationship. We had been dating for almost two years by then.

I thought back to the first time I met Bianca, about a year before Romero died. I didn't realize he was planning on asking me to move in with him, which he did after that, or that he would ask me to marry him, which he did the last time after we made love. Anyhow, we'd spent the day at the Santa Monica beach and she turned out to be a cool kid.

Now, something about going to church made me feel like I should reach out to Romero's daughter, Bianca. I was feeling like I had failed her. I really wished I had met her more, spent more time with her, but I was so into building my business I didn't. Also, I made it clear to Romero, I wasn't a stepmother type. He'd surprised me the day we picked Bianca up, and he later told me, "I am so happy Bianca likes you."

"This is Zipporah Saldano. I was Romero's fiancée. I was just calling to see how Bianca was doing?"

The other end of the line was silent. "She's fine." Jade's voice was curt.

"I know it has to be hard for her to have lost her father."

"Yes, she took it hard." She still sounded brusque. She continued in a cold tone, "We were high school sweethearts, and I must give it to him, he was a good father. Now I don't know about as a husband. He was married to that job. But that's all right. I am remarried and I am doing fine."

"Good . . . I was wondering if I could see Bianca sometimes?"

Jade didn't answer right away. "No, I don't think that will be a good idea. Y'all weren't married. From what I heard, you caused his death. Please don't call here anymore."

She hung up before I could explain and without saying good-bye.

Crushed, I sat in my car, not knowing how to react. I felt hurt when she was so abrupt with me at the beginning of the conversation, but this was a blow.

I really wanted to spend some time with Bianca. But, then I thought about it. Maybe it was for the best—for now.

I guessed I was being delusional to think Jade would welcome me with open arms. To think, I'd been planning to ask her if she knew Romero's blood type or if she knew Bianca's blood type; that was suicidal. She would have become suspicious and wanted to know why I wanted to know. I hated to think it, but I was glad I missed that bullet. I didn't want anyone to know I had doubts about the paternity.

I knew with the advances in DNA you could even tell the paternity of a child while you were pregnant, but I'd decided not to get the test, so here I was. Back where I started.

Chapter Sixteen

"Great show!" Zara Pickett, the executive producer, said as we walked off the temporary set at Wolfgang Puck's Spago restaurant in Beverly Hills for our last show of the season. We had already shot six weeks' worth of unscripted shows and were already slated for a second season. We wouldn't shoot for another six months, and I figured I'd have the baby while we were on break, before we began to shoot our next season.

Most of the shows had been shot at Haviland's mini-mansion in Hollywood Hills and our office in Santa Monica. We had been getting a lot of press because of the show, as well. *Women in Business* had been featured in *Ebony, Jet, Black Enterprise,* and other, smaller magazines; plus, we were scheduled to be showcased in *Essence* and *Oprah* in the next six months.

I took off my mic, and made it to the bathroom in time to upchuck my breakfast of a vegetarian omelet. Although I wasn't really showing yet, I

was going into my twenty-sixth week of pregnancy and still had morning sickness. I didn't
have it as often as I did before though. Maybe
that was why I didn't really look pregnant. My
obstetrics doctor, Gail Henderson, told me I
needed to gain more weight. I was on a regimen
of strong prenatal vitamins and extra iron pills.
Once a week, I was given an iron shot in the hip.

In an earlier shot this week the cameramen
had followed me in my quest to find missing
baby Kyle, who we renamed Tara. We reenacted
the case to protect the privacy of the family
members and the people involved. Also, because
of the confidentiality clause for minors, we could
not show the actual child.

The white actors who played the parents,
two professional lawyers, were devastated and
almost, but not quite, captured the pathos of
parents of a missing child. Fortunately, I was
able to track the toddler down with the nanny
and her undocumented immigrant husband
from Nigeria.

I showed how I backtracked to the last few
places the nanny was seen, checked where she'd
last used her debit card, and found her hiding
out in a Marriot Hotel. The baby actress was unharmed, and it gave the audience a good example
of the behind-the-scenes things done for missing

children. The actors simulated how the missing children division of LAPD arrested the nanny and the husband and how the baby was safely returned to her relieved yet stressed-out parents.

Next, the cameramen had also followed Chica on a bounty hunting quest, where she'd found a skinhead defendant named Snake who'd jumped bail. Chica, who was as tough as nails, wrestled down her defendant as easily as any man.

But our tracking expertise wasn't what fired up the viewership. No, what made the Nielsen ratings needle sing was Haviland. The audience was more interested in that crazy fool and how she dogged out her man. Judging from the ratings, the audience loved the drama. Talk about a train wreck of a relationship.

I tried to lie back and relax on one of the two love seats provided in our trailer. Chica came in after me and put her hand on my forehead to see if I was feeling okay.

"You looked flushed, *mija*."

"I may need your help, Chica," I said. Chica was a hotspur—a loose cannon—and I knew she'd handle this.

"Shoot."

"I have someone trying to blackmail me."

"Say what?" Chica started cursing in Ricky Ricardo Spanish.

"Calm down, Chica. I'll tell you about it later. At least I have good news."

"Yeah, that was good about you and your mom, the boys, and your sister having such a nice reunion. Have you talked to your sister?"

"Every week. We're getting closer. She's a sweetheart."

"Do you think you would want to add your family reunion on the show?"

"No, I'm too private. I don't know how Keyshia Cole did it with how her family was always showing out."

"I loved how she had so much love for Frankie and her family members," Chica objected. "It made me respect Keyshia as a human being. I didn't just see her as a celebrity."

"That part was all right. But the world loves to see how ignorant some of our families are." I shook my head. I washed my hands up and down together. "Thanks but no thanks! Not to play the slavery card, but what can you expect when you take people away from their culture, and sell them away from their family members like they did the Africans? It's a wonder we're not more dysfunctional than we are. For real, though, we are still feeling the effects of posttraumatic slavery disorder in a lot of our families. Sometimes I think maybe we are just doing the best we can do."

Chica looked down and softly touched my stomach. "I see you're showing a little bit." She looked pleased to know I hadn't terminated the pregnancy. "Look at my little niece or nephew."

I glanced down. "Oh, this little pudge?" I blushed, brushing it off. I'd been wearing loose dark tops and jackets to cover up the pregnancy. I wasn't exactly ready to announce it on the show.

"So Romero left you his house?" Chica remarked in a desultory manner.

Shirley and she were the only ones I'd told about my windfall. I nodded. "I moved in last weekend."

"*Mija*, I would have helped you. Why didn't you tell me? You know you don't need to be lifting with the baby and all."

"I really didn't have much to take. Just Ben, my clothes, and my laptop. His place is already furnished." Sometimes I found myself still talking about Romero in the present tense.

I glanced up to see Haviland standing in the doorway. I put my fingers to my lips for Chica to hush when I saw big-mouth Haviland floating up behind her into the trailer we all shared. I could see she was trying to ear hustle. She had a penchant for always showing up at the last minute so she could get into our conversation. Chica and I both worked with criminals and we often discussed our cases without including Haviland, whose wedding planning clientele included the A list of Beverly Hills actors and actresses.

"Hey, girlfriend," Haviland said, both hands waving in the air, painting word pictures as they usually did. "I swear, I'm PMSing again, and I'm afraid I'll kill Trevor. If he whines one more time to me, 'Hav, baby, what did I do?' I'm going to let him have it." She missed her calling as a comedienne, and was able to do a good impression of Trevor, too.

Haviland flopped down on the other love seat the production company had in our trailer which acted as our dressing room.

I got up and went and sat in front of the dressing room vanity mirror. I stuck a piece of tissue in a jar of cold cream. "TMI," I said, wiping off my makeup. "You're giving too much information again, Haviland."

"I know. Did I give up too much of our business when I talked about our sex life?"

"Yes, you did." Sometimes I can be too blunt.

"Well, stop me."

"I tried. Didn't you see me take my finger and cut my throat, telling you to shut up?"

"I guess I'm just being anal again. I can't stop once I get started. I know I'm such a control freak. Trevor drives me crazy with how slow he is and just how he does things. Besides, this is helping his acting career and I'm the one who pitched the show. He says I'm acting too 'hoity-toity' now. Can you believe that?"

"No, you're just OCD," I teased. "And, just like anyone with an obsessive-compulsive disorder, you like everything in its place. You over clean. I've seen you even wash your plant leaves. You can't control people, places, or things. Lighten up on Trevor. He's a good guy."

Chica jumped in, changing the subject. "Have you told her yet?" She lifted her eyebrow and glanced down at my stomach. I knew she was referring to my pregnancy.

"Told me what?" Haviland's nose quivered with curiosity.

I shook my head. "Not now."

"Pretty please, tell me." Haviland jumped off the love seat. "You two are keeping secrets from me again?"

"You know you can't hold water with your big mouth," I quipped. I wasn't being mean. This was the God's truth. Haviland couldn't hold a secret if it meant it would save her own life. I was beginning to accept this about Haviland as one of her weaknesses. Although I didn't trust her as far as I could see her, I was beginning to like her a little more. She was moving from the frenemy scale to the low end of the friendship continuum, if there was such a thing.

"I swear on my dead mother's grave I won't say anything." Haviland licked her index finger and pointed it up to the ceiling.

Really, Haviland? I thought. *You only knew your biological mother a month before she died from AIDS and now you're always swearing on her grave.* I didn't say anything though. I know Haviland is a trip.

"See. I never told anyone when you went out the country. By the way, you never told me what happened while you were gone either. I'm tired of how you and Chica are always talking in some secret language that is not Spanish either because I know that ish."

"We grew up together," Chica said in our defense. "That's our version of pig Latin and Spanglish."

"What are you not telling me then?"

I started not to tell her but something in me said, *what the heck?* "I'm pregnant, now." I blurted it out. I added the "now," as if I were a kid saying in a dare, "Now there."

Haviland started jumping up and down, screaming in excitement. "OMG. Why didn't you tell me? I'll be the best godmother in the world." She threw her arms around me in a claustrophobic hug.

She continued. "Girl, you got chutzpah." Haviland—who spoke Spanish, French, and Japanese fluently, as her adoptive family traveled worldwide while she was growing up—always dropped Yiddish words in her conversation since she'd been raised around Jewish grandparents. "I don't think I could ever have a baby. Let alone be a single mother. I'm too selfish. But you'll be the best mother in the world, I just know it."

I peeled her arms from around me, feeling embarrassed, but, at the same time, somehow happy she was so excited.

"Tell me about that book deal you've gotten with Simon & Schuster because of the show," I said, changing the subject. "You generally can't hold a secret, but I see you held that close to your vest." I gave her a piercing look, since I'd seen the information online on a blog. Oddly, Haviland didn't share that tidbit of information with me or Chica.

Haviland calmed down and started using her hands again. "It's going to be a memoir about my life as a child actor. You have more of a story to tell than me, Z, but you're so private.

"Well, anyhow, how about the *Essence* article they're doing on all three of us regarding the show?" Haviland reminded me. "They're going to do a beautiful photo shoot. To me, that's win-win. I'm not trying to hog the spotlight. I think we've all benefited."

Who is the "we" in this case? I wondered.

"True. Look, I'm happy for you," I conceded.

"This is for all of us. We're all going to make money. "

"Well, I'm glad we're through shooting for this season. I'm planning on taking the rest of this time off for my maternity leave."

"How far are you?" Haviland asked.

"I'm just going into my sixth month."

"You're not even showing." She gently touched my stomach.

Suddenly the baby gave a strong kick and Haviland withdrew her hand.

She let out a yelp. "What was that?"

"That's the baby kicking—silly. Haven't you ever felt—"

"Zipporah Saldano, Can we speak to you?" A voice interrupted our conversation.

I glanced up. Two suits framed the doorway to our trailer. One officer was black and one was white. I always knew the law, even when they didn't wear uniforms. "Who are you?"

"LAPD. I'm Detective Steve Mitchell. This is Detective Lionel Patterson. We'd like to take you down to the morgue to see if you can identify a body."

My heart started pounding immediately. Was this Mayhem's body? *Oh, Lord, no!* As much as I declared to my mother I didn't care what happened to my brother, I couldn't bear the thought of anything happening to him. I hadn't heard from him since he went to Rio almost three months ago. He'd been gone with no word. Was he safe? Was he even alive?

Chapter Seventeen

On the drive to the city morgue, I got a text message:

> We are going to move on this. We want $500,000 dollars by the end of the week. We mean business.

I thought about how Mayhem said that he'd paid the two agents off. And what if it wasn't Agent Braggs and Agent Jerry Stamper? Then who could it be?

A second text came in:

> Meet us at Universal Studios at the brand new 5 Towers on Saturday at 3:00 P.M. Bring the money in unmarked bills.

Who is the us? I wondered. Today was Wednesday.

On the ride I was reminded of how I was swooped up from the Academy Awards by the two crooked Feds when they'd set up Mayhem's kidnapping. What was going on?

The Los Angeles County Department of the Coroner is located north of downtown L.A. on Mission Road.

As they drove, I wondered if these two detectives were in cahoots with the crooked federal agents responsible for Mayhem's kidnapping. Did these detectives know I had left Tank's sawed-off head in the Santa Monica park? Were they the ones with the video of me dropping off the basket? The video also included the opening of the basket, which showed Tank's head.

If anything, were they the ones who murdered Tank? Had the blackmailer(s) dropped the dime on me? My heart was beating erratically. Was it my brother's body in the morgue? I hadn't heard back from him. Was he safe? Did he go to Rio alone?

The unmarked car finally stopped. When we went inside the building, I suddenly felt the icy fingers of death touch me in my soul. Now I was coming face-to-face with the lie I told when I was rushing to Rio.

"Why am I here?" I asked, trying to sound innocent. I tried to keep my face straight, and hide my fear. I was scared to death. Did they know I knew about the decapitated head?

"We have an unidentified decedent who we think you can identify," Detective Mitchell said.

My heart palpitated. I felt like I was walking through a tomb as I trudged through the cold corridors. I guessed I was in a tomb.

We walked inside the coroner's examining room, and they took me to a large walk-in refrigerator that stored other bodies. They pulled the sheet back on a headless, handless, and footless body. I gasped.

"Do you know who this is?"

"No."

"We don't believe you."

"Why?"

"We had an anonymous tip that you might know who beheaded this person."

Just seeing the corpse, it almost made me regurgitate again. Tank used to remind me of the late actor Michael Clarke Duncan. This body was that of a big male, about six feet six. I could see the bullet hole in his left bicep so that was the identifying mark for me, but I acted like I'd never seen him before. Even his feet were missing, but I guessed that was the way they gave proof that the hit was done. *Who put the hit out on Tank?*

I'd observed that when I went and got the information as to where his sister lived, who had the boys, in order to help get my nephews out of L.A. One side of me was relieved that it wasn't Mayhem. But the other side was grieved but happy that they had found Tank's body.

Now where was his head? His hands? His feet? I remembered seeing on *NCIS* that the cartels paid a hit man to do a job and the hit man would have to cut off the feet as proof of delivering the job, and cut off the hands to hide the fingerprints. I don't know what the cutting off of the head was to signify. I wondered.

They say the dead don't lie. I could hear Tank's voice mocking me: *"I deserve to have my head with my body."*

"What?"

I took a deep breath. "No, I don't know who he is."

"Well, we want to put you in a lineup. We have someone who says otherwise."

From there I was taken over to Parker Center.

Chapter Eighteen

I'd never been in jail before, but it had to rank as one of the worst experiences I'd ever lived through. They claimed I was identified in the lineup as one of the last to be seen with Tank, aka Andre Clinton, so here I was arrested and thrown in jail with what I considered little or no probable cause. I had no idea what the charges were going to be against me, or how long I'd be incarcerated.

We were squeezed, almost like sardines, in a holding pen, which was about twenty by twenty. The smells were so rank, so rancid, I tried to breathe the air through an imaginary little O in my mouth to cut down on the strength of the smell. In between every other breath, I tried to ease oxygen out of one nostril, and then the other. It wasn't working though.

I was surrounded by prostitutes, boosters, murderers, and younger women who had probably gotten caught up carrying drugs for their boyfriends. One Amazonian woman named Big Red swaggered around the cell, very stud-like, pants sagging, as if she owned the place. She was at least six feet two. She had the cinderblock face of a man, broad shoulders like a linebacker, and feet that were at least a size thirteen. She wore red dreadlocks, which hung down her back.

"Hey." Big Red came over and stood over me, sniffing like a dog in heat, on the prowl, but also ready to attack.

I knew I had to get her off me, yet not make her feel dissed. "Hey." I kept my game face on. I refused to be intimidated. I was thinking about my tae kwon do, but at the same time, I knew I couldn't be out here fighting when I was pregnant.

I could tell "Tree," as I nicknamed her inwardly, was itching for a fight. I'm five feet nine, but she was even taller.

"Wassup?"

I nodded in acknowledgment of her greeting.

"What'chu in here for?" she grunted.

I just gave her a look.

"You trying to diss me?" Big Red puffed up her chest, balled up her fist, and was ready to fire on me. Her face was set in hard lines.

I could tell from her tattoo that she was a Crip also.

I had an idea. "You know Big Homie who owns Kitty Kat Koliseum? He 8 Tray." The truth be known I didn't know what set Mayhem currently was in, but I knew the street gang names for the different Crips sets from growing up in a Crip family, and from learning the gang set identifications through the police academy training.

"Yeah, I know Big Homie. Who on the street don't know him?"

"He my brother." I purposely spoke in Ebonics to let her know we both were from the same tribe—the tribe of crazy.

A look of fear flashed across Big Red's face. Unwillingly, she unfurled her fist. I could literally see each finger ease out of her fist, she moved in such slow motion. "Oh, yeah."

I watched her visibly shrink back and get out of my personal space, if there was such a thing when you were on lockdown in a crowded cell of women.

Big Red starting speaking in a congenial tone. "Homegirl, welcome to the Taj Mahal." She turned to the other predatory women in the cage. "Hey, all y'all bitches up in here. Word up. Y'all see homegirl here. Nobody bet' not mess with her. She fam'. Her brother is Big Homie."

All the women from the hookers to the mules to the dealers to the junkies nodded in silent assent. The rapacious gaze that was always seeking "who is the one to be abused" turned to a terrified look mixed with one of deference on their faces. I was glad they realized now that I was not "the one" to be played with. The women started acting extra nice toward me.

"Hey, get off that bench, and let homegirl sit down."

For the first time, I was glad that Mayhem was my big brother. It was like having a legal guardian angel straight from the pits of hell. Satan, who could appear as an angel of mercy but who was also an angel of darkness. But now I was beginning to wonder if Mayhem was as bad as he was made out to be. What was that he had said about the secret society that made him seem like a saint?

I eased out a sigh of relief. I sat down and tried to act normal, but I couldn't stand it. I had hand sanitizer with me, and I kept using it. I could see what looked like green puss running out of one of the junkie's arms. I prayed I didn't catch anything.

Somehow, I managed not to have a bowel movement, but I couldn't help urinating. As a courtesy for almost messing with Big Homie's people, Big Red would stand with her back to me and cover me up. There was only one toilet and it stank to high heaven.

Now I had an idea of how Venita must have felt in jail, then later in prison while she was pregnant. Powerless. Hopeless. Helpless. Pregnancy is the world's most vulnerable place a woman can ever find herself. I don't care if she's got the best husband in the world, she has to carry this baby by herself. She's so attuned to the universe, she can feel, smell, taste everything around her. She is more sensitive to the world because she is now in touch with God. But, to be caged like an animal, now that had to be one of the worst things that could happen to a woman.

I thought about what Venita said about having a baby in prison was her lowest point, and I really became afraid. I didn't want to have my baby while I was in prison. *Oh, Lord, help me!* What were the charges they had against me?

I promised myself if I got out of there, I would never go back to jail.

Chapter Nineteen

Two days later, charges were dropped and I was released. They had held me the legal forty-eight hours, but I felt it had been an illegal hold. I'd never had such an awful experience in my life as the two nights I spent in jail. In California, the law can keep you up to forty-eight hours without having an official charge until the prosecuting office filed charges.

I didn't know who to call. I was too ashamed to call Chica or Haviland, although last year I'd gotten Haviland out of jail for unpaid tickets. I didn't want to burden Shirley, whose plate was full.

I'd never felt so vulnerable in my adult life, but now I knew what it was to feel powerless. If I got a felony, I'd never be able to vote, or to keep my license as a private investigator. I vowed now that I would have to clear my name. I knew I was innocent, but Black people went to prison all the time for crimes they didn't commit. Nelson

Mandela. Rubin "Hurricane" Carter. Angela Davis. And they were famous, so who cared if I went to prison for life since I wasn't really a celebrity?

I couldn't even say, "Oh, that will never happen to me," and feel comfortable. Then what would happen to my baby? Oh, Lord, I was going to have to get to the bottom of this mess. I didn't want to be part of the new slave system—mass incarceration.

Finally, I got my telephone call and I called Venita. Thank God she was at home and answered on the second ring. She accepted the charges from an inmate.

"Venita. I've been arrested. The prosecutor didn't file charges so I'm being released. Can you pick me up from L.A. County?"

"Oh, Z, my goodness! Sure, I'll be right there. I have a car now."

Booking returned my purse, and I was able to cut on my cell phone. While I waited for Venita, I received another text message: We're serious. Next time, we'll have the charges filed. We want $1 million now.

I had never been happier to see Venita in my life when she showed up to get me released. I didn't get a sigh of relief out, though, until we walked out the jail and I got my first taste of *freedom*. My hair was nappy and I was funky. I hadn't brushed my teeth in two days. But I was free. Even the air tasted better.

"Where do you want to go?"

"Home. I live in Silver Lake now."

"Do you want to talk about what happened?"

"It's related to what happened when I was investigating and trying to help Mayhem."

"What was that?"

"I can't tell you right now, but I've got to investigate it. It seems like someone's trying to set me up."

One thing I can say is that Venita didn't throw it up in my face about my going to jail. I knew she was upset, but she only offered support.

Once Venita pulled up to my house, I invited her in. I'd never had her to my place since she'd been released from jail three years ago. I guess I felt I could now trust her. I opened the door and for the first time, I saw how my spot must have looked as it filtered through Venita's eyes. It was a masculine house—it still had all Romero's camel leather sectional furniture. The oak floors were dull because they hadn't been waxed. The drapes, which darkened the room like a casket, were chocolate. The place looked dark, which was still how I felt most days.

"This is a nice house. Just needs some tender loving care," Venita said.

While I took my shower, washed my hair, and brushed my teeth, Venita picked up my house, which was cluttered in the living room, where I worked on my laptop. She opened the curtains and all the windows, dusted the framed pictures on the fireplace of Romero and me on our trip to Santa Barbara and Palm Springs when I was in hiding during my investigation of Trayvon's murder. She had also opened Ben's cage and cleaned it out and let him out.

By the time I came out the bathroom, I found Venita in the small Mexican-looking turquoise-painted kitchen. She had cooked a simple meal of quesadillas with chopped-up tomatoes, cilantro, and black olives, and some fried hash brown potatoes with onions. My refrigerator was practically empty, so it was ingenious how she came up with that meal at all. She'd taken lemons off the tree in the backyard and made a large Mason jar of lemonade. The house had an airy lightness to it that I hadn't felt since I'd moved in. She had opened the windows and let out some of the grief.

The smells were tantalizing and comforting. For the first time since my mother had gotten out of jail, I felt happy to have her back in my life. "How did you find all this food when I didn't have that much in the refrigerator?"

"I'm a woman. Girl, we are magical. We can do whatever we have to do with whatever we have."

I smiled as we sat down to eat. Once again, holding my hands, Venita prayed before we ate. "Father God, Allah, thank you for getting my child released. Let her name—Zipporah I Love Saldano—be cleared of all charges. Let her keep her record, clean. Amen."

"Amen." Now I really was in need of prayer.

I didn't trust Venita when she first was released from prison, but slowly I was feeling a trust come back for her. After all, who else could I run to? Shirley's plate was filled with the four teenage girls and Daddy Chill, with his dementia.

After we finished eating, we sat down in the living room. Venita went out in my front yard and cut a piece of Birds of Paradise. She took another Mason jar and made a center piece.

"I never knew you were this creative, Venita," I commented.

"I did a lot of arts and crafts in prison. They developed a garden and that's how I fell in love with plants and flowers. That's what helped the time go by."

I didn't say anything. It was still hard to reconcile the old "OG" Crip mother with this new nurturing, creative woman.

"I'm not trying to get in your business, Z, but he seems like someone special to you, judging from the pictures I've seen." Venita's words interrupted my thoughts. She pointed toward the pictures on the fireplace.

That's when I realized I hadn't ever told Venita about Romero. "He was."

"What do you mean . . . was?"

"He's dead."

"What? I'm so sorry to hear that. What happened to him?"

I took a deep breath and told her the entire story from how we met when I was eighteen, during the L.A. riots, when he kept me from getting gang raped, to how he came back into my life after I was shot on the LAPD. I told her how he gave me the card for the rehabilitation program I went into, which helped me get sober and saved my life. I told her about my murder investigation case with Trayvon and how I came here to hide out, how we became more than friends. I told her how Romero asked me to marry him, and, up to the point of me going off to Brazil without telling him, so I could free Mayhem, how the two of us were inseparable. Finally, I told her how he got shot trying to help me free Mayhem and save me.

Tears filled Venita's eyes. "Romero sounds like he really loved you."

"Yes, Romero did. I didn't even believe in love when he came into my life. But he showed me what love was. Anyhow, he left this house to me. Maybe he felt something bad was going to happen once he got involved with keeping his family from killing Mayhem . . . I don't know. I just found out about the house when I heard his message on my voice mail. He'd left the message three months ago, just before he died. I had never listened to my messages."

"That's something. He helped free my son . . ." Venita's voice dropped off in a tone of disbelief. I guessed she knew from experience now not to seem too happy about Mayhem around me. I was trying not to be so jealous so I forgave the tears of joy I saw in her eyes. "God bless his soul."

A hush fell over the room. Finally I spoke up. "I have something to tell you . . . Good news."

"What is it?"

"I think I've found Daniel, Diggity."

"Are you kidding me?"

"No, I'm serious. He's a sergeant in the Army. He's deployed in Iraq. He sent me an e-mail."

Venita's hands flew to her mouth to keep from screaming. Her eyes watered. "This is wonderful. I'm so glad he's alive. That he's not in any type of trouble."

"I know . . . I had worried too with him being a Black male." I thought of what had almost become a normal eventuality for too many young Black males: the prison, or the graveyard. That's sad, but I believed that little Diggity beat the odds and had turned out fine. He hadn't become a statistic. Like the writer Antwone Fisher, he sounded as if the service had helped make a man out of him. "I haven't heard back from him since the first e-mail, but I'm hoping."

"Is there anything else you would like to tell me?" Venita peered at me with a searching look. I could tell by her gaze that she knew.

"Yes . . . I'm pregnant."

"I knew it. Hallelujah!" Venita grabbed me, kissed my cheek, and hugged me all up. "I've been dreaming fish for the past few months. I dreamed you had a baby boy, but when you dream it, sometimes it's the opposite. It would be nice if you have a daughter."

For the first time, I relaxed into my mother's hug. On a deep level, I felt like a baby in its mother's arms. My heart leaped and soared. I had to pull away before I crawled back up in the womb.

"Thanks, Venita."

I felt better now that I had told Venita. Generally, Shirley will tell Venita things about me, but I guessed my foster mother felt this was something I should tell her myself.

The other good thing was Venita took Ben home with her. She said the boys would enjoy playing with him.

After she left, I thought about how, regardless of whether I wanted to admit it or not, Venita had shaped my most formative years. Part of who I was today was because of her. I was thinking of how Venita was the type of mother who made you go and fight for yourself.

A memory, long buried, surfaced. I remembered when I was about eight years old a classmate named Shawana was threatening to beat me up. Part of the nonsensical reason was because Venita dressed me to the nines, thanks to children's clothes bought from the local booster. She also kept my hair neatly combed and braided in the nicest intricate styles with matching barrettes.

Now don't get me wong. There was a time in the projects when most little Black girls had their hair neatly combed and dressed. But with the crack epidemic in the eighties, more and more little girls were beginning to look like vagabonds, if Big Mommas or aunties didn't step in and help.

When I was a child, people wouldn't just comment on my clean appearance, they would look at me and say, "You really have such long hair and are so pretty to be dark skinned."

Talk about a collective cultural, psychological scar of a people when it came to hair and color, but that's another issue.

Now, although my tormentor was probably my age, she was much taller and thicker than I was. Obviously, Shawana's mother was on crack and this child was never dressed as nicely as I was. Worse, she knew I was afraid of her. For whatever reason, she spent that particular day at school kicking the back of my desk. "When school lets out, I'ma beat your ass," she kept hissing.

Fights were common in our hood. It wasn't that I went for bad, it's just I never had to fight because of who my family was. Up until then, I'd been protected by association with Mayhem. Unfortunately, by then, though, my brother, at the age of nine, missed more school than he attended, so I couldn't run to him for protection.

I was sweating bullets, stressed out, and quaking in my shoes all that day. The hands on the clock seemed to creep and crawl until it was time for school to let out. I couldn't wait for the bell to ring and school to dismiss. As soon as it did, I hauled ass home, with Shawana and her crew hot on my heels.

As soon as Venita saw me when I crossed the threshold of our project unit, she knew something was wrong. She looked up from the ironing board where she was ironing one of my many outfits. "What the hell is the matter with you, girl?" she hollered, which was how she communicated most of the time, talking loud and cussing.

Tears muffled in my voice, I blurted out, "Shawana say she gon' beat me up."

"Where she at?"

"She outside."

Venita looked out the door and saw the crowd of children waiting for a fight. I wanted her to go out and fight my battle for me, but she pushed me back outside. "Go out there and fight that heffa. Even if she beat yo' ass, you better fight her back. If you don't fight her back, I'm a beat yo' ass myself. Don't you ever run your narrow ass in here scared of nobody."

I went out and fought Shawana with everything I had inside of me. Somehow, I won, by whatever standard street fights were solved, and from then on, I was never picked on or bullied. When Mayhem found out about it, he took me out to the park and taught me how to handle a gun—which was how I was such a good shot when I went through the LAPD Police Academy years later.

I guessed, in her crazy way, Venita had shown me love. So I thought about the lesson Venita taught me that day: never back down from no one. Pregnant or not, it was time for me to get busy, but I didn't know how long I'd be gone when I had to go dig into the sewers of the street.

Chapter Twenty

After Venita left, I called Mayhem's cell phone. I was surprised when he answered on the third ring. He'd been gone over three months and I was really becoming worried. He was getting ready to board the plane in Rio, headed back to the United States.

"Are you all right?" I asked.

"I'm good."

"Did you find Appolonia?"

He became quiet. "No. It's a long story . . . . What's happenin'?"

I blurted it out. "I'm about to be blackmailed by these two fools—Agent Braggs and Agent Stamper. They're still asking for another million."

"Don't give them shit . . . Fuck them. I already paid them bitches. What are they trying to blackmail you for anyway?"

"They set me up. I've been locked up behind them. They're trying to blackmail me about Tank."

"Why would they do that?"

I caught myself. I had lied to Mayhem and now I'd have to come clean. "It's a long story. I'll tell you when you get back."

"You still got the password. If you need to, go and take the money. I'll take care of them when I get back."

I didn't want to use Mayhem's services and be obligated to him. I had another idea. I hadn't really gone and thoroughly searched the house since I'd moved back in a few weeks ago. I mainly worked in the living room and even slept in there on the let-out sofa. I wasn't strong enough yet to sleep on the same sheets we'd slept on. Although the sheets looked clean, I could tell they hadn't been changed since Romero died. They still smelled like Romero and, although I didn't sleep on them, I wasn't ready to change them.

I wanted to keep all the sweaters he had, all his uniforms, which hadn't been cleaned, even his old threadbare robe, just so I could go in and smell them for comfort. I went and checked his dresser drawer and found my engagement ring in the box. I put it on the chain around my neck with the amulet.

For the first time, I went into Romero's home office and checked his laptop, which, unfortunately, had a password. I didn't know his password. I paused for a moment. Something told me to try my name. I typed in "Zipporah," and bingo, I was into his laptop. As to be expected, Romero's files were very organized. I was looking for his partner's phone number, which I found in alphabetical order under his file named "Contacts." I found Detective Mitchell Hamilton's phone number under "Partner."

I programmed his phone number into my iPhone. I called and introduced myself. "Hello, my name is Zipporah Saldano—I was a friend of Romero's."

"Sure. I know of you. You're Z . . . Romero's fiancée," Detective Hamilton said in a jovial tone. "You were all he talked about. He wanted to marry you. He showed me the ring he bought you. I can't believe he's gone. He was a good guy."

"Sure was."

"Can we meet around four o' clock today? This is urgent."

"Yes. Let's meet at the old Forum in Inglewood."

First, I went to Bank of America downtown and went into Mayhem's safe deposit box. I was surprised that there was no jewelry or bling inside. No cash. All I found was a large manila envelope. I opened it and took out a flash drive. I also left the two flash drives with Mayhem's accounts in the safe deposit box for safety. I didn't need the money. I'd saved money over the past two years, and the money from the show had been banked as well.

Afterward, I sat in my car, going over the information on my new iPad. The list of crooked agents included the two federal agents, Special Agent Jerry Stamper, FBI, and Special Agent Richard Braggs, DEA, who had set up my brother's kidnapping. They both had been involved in shaking down drug dealers, not turning in drugs when they confiscated them, and had green-lighted a few street hits between the Mexican and Black gangs.

There was also information on a secret society called The White Falcons. The main mission of this group was to take back over and return White men to power. They hated the fact that President Obama had been elected for another term. They wanted to regain power by white supremacy by any means necessary. There was a list that sounded like possible green lights against various Black political leaders. There were bribes to judges to set cases against Black political prisoners. *Whew!* I let out a deep breath. How did Mayhem get this information? No wonder they wanted him dead.

I drove from downtown to Inglewood to the Forum parking lot. On the drive there, I kept looking back, seeing shadows in the corner of my eyes, in my rearview mirror. As soon as I pulled up, I saw the unmarked pewter-colored detective car.

I was surprised to find out that Romero's old partner was a white dude. He looked to be about thirty-something. He had narrow, closely set eyes and plain brown hair. He reminded me of Ethan Hawke, who played Jake in *Training Day*. I guess I was only surprised because I'd always assumed he was a Hispanic fellow officer. They both always spoke in Spanish over the phone whenever he called the house and they talked, as well as they had both become fluent in Vietnamese and Korean. L.A. was a multicultural gumbo, so most of the detectives were not only bilingual, they were trilingual.

I'd never really met him and I thought it was because Romero kept his private life separate from the job. I showed him my identification and Detective Hamilton showed me his.

"What did you want to talk about that you couldn't tell me on the phone?" Detective Hamilton asked.

"Are you wearing a wire?" That was my first question.

"No, I'm straight." I frisked him anyhow and he was clean. "I don't know who I can turn to, or who I can trust," I began, "but I know Romero trusted you with his life."

"True dat."

"Well, I'm coming to you as Romero's friend because this is about corruption in the DEA and the FBI."

I had already devised a plan in the back of my mind to entrap these two. I related what had happened and showed him the text messages that did not include any incriminating information on me. I climbed into his car and fired up my laptop. Out of the corner of my eyes, I studied Detective Hamilton's face as it crumpled into ridges of alarm as he read deeper into the documents.

After a long silence, I interjected, "I have a three P.M. meeting with them at Universal Studios at the new Tower."

"Go ahead and have the meeting."

"Are you in?"

"Fo'sho. Can you wear a wire?"

"No problem."

"I'll come with my new partner, and we'll be nearby. Act as if you're taking them the money, though. Come to the station and we'll give you some real, marked bills to have on top and some fake money. I'll also have backup with me. You have my cell phone number, so we can text."

I gave him a copy of the flash drive with the information I had on Agent Braggs and Agent Stamper and the others. After he thought about it, he let out a low whistle in kind of an Ooohweee melody. "This can be dangerous information. Be careful." His face drained all of its color and he definitely seemed a little shaken.

"Meet us at twelve P.M. at West L.A. station and we'll get you fitted up for a wire."

"Will you follow me?"

"Definitely. You just meet them, and I'll be right behind you. Why do they want to blackmail you?"

I told him about their attempts to blackmail me because of my brother's kidnapping. I left out the part about my getting Tank's head in the mail and dumping it in the park.

"I'll tell you what we'll do. I'll get a squad to follow us out there." He let out a long deep breath. "We'll catch them," Detective Hamilton assured me.

As soon as he drove off, I called Chica, and told her what I wanted her to do.

"Gotcha, *mija*."

Chapter Twenty-one

I drove over to the West LAPD station and met with Detective Hamilton, where I was fitted with an electronic wire. Part of it was in my ear. It was much smaller than the old wires they used when I was on the job. I pulled my hair over my ear.

I put in a call to Chica, who'd done a stakeout at Agent Braggs's house last night.

"He's leaving now," she whispered into the phone. "In fact, Agent Jerry Stamper just pulled up to his house and they are riding in separate cars. They both packing, *mija*. Be careful."

"You too."

I arrived an hour early at Universal so I could see if my blackmailers were, in fact, Agent Richard Braggs and Agent Jerry Stamper. I carried a briefcase with the top bills that were real. They covered fake money provided by Detective Hamilton. Back up was sitting around the park in plain clothes. They'd all driven in unmarked cars.

I didn't see but a few people in the area, and the usual crowds were missing.

"Testing, testing, one, two, three, can you hear me?" Detective Hamilton was calling my name over my wire.

"You're coming in loud and clear. Do you see the perps yet?"

"Not yet."

It was a foggy day and the Studios weren't as crowded as they usually was. You really couldn't see but a few feet in front of you. The frigid dampness in the air pierced me to the bone.

I stood by the Tower, waiting. I was beginning to get a little cold, and I felt my baby kicking. Whenever I became anxious, the baby would move around and around.

Just when I was about to give up on them showing up, I saw the two men heading for me. As they got closer I saw it was Glass Eye and Agent Stamper.

"I see you're here," Glass Eye, aka Special Agent Richard Braggs, stated rhetorically. Standing in the fog, he really looked like the devil. I wondered what made him cross the line to the dark side.

"Why have you been following me?" I said, trying to get them to admit to as much as possible on tape. "My brother said he paid you."

"Yes, he did. We just wanted you to know we mean business, too. But we've got another person who's gotten involved and he's gotten greedy. He wants $500,000 and we want the other $500,000 for our finder's fee."

"Why did y'all set up my brother's kidnapping?"

His lips curled into a look of distaste. "Fuck your brother. He's collateral damage as far as we're concerned. Ninja got where he thought he wasn't going to pay his taxes to us . . . . He really had gotten it twisted."

"What happened to Tank—my brother's lieutenant?"

"Just say he was collateral damage too."

I paused. This was just as good as a confession. So they probably did order the hit on Tank to shake me up and make me go to Brazil to get the money.

"So why are you trying to set me up?"

"Like I say, we got an outside interested party. Besides, you're a liability."

I let that digest for a moment. So the blackmailers were being blackmailed.

"Where's the video?"

They handed me a flashdrive and I handed over the brief case. Just as Agent Braggs opened it, I gave the code words "Now is that enough?"

so the LAPD could come rushing in and arrest these fools.

Without warning, though, shots pierced the air. Right before my eyes, Agent Braggs crumpled to the ground, and, in a flash, Agent Stamper grabbed the briefcase out of Agent Bragg's bloody hands, and dashed off. I looked down and saw that Agent Braggs had been hit. Who was the shooter? I hid for cover and pulled out my piece. However, the shots were not from the direction that the police team was situated in an unassuming van or from the under cover cops who were sprinkled throughout the lots.

I dropped to the floor and just moved behind the inside of the doorway. I decided not to shoot back because I didn't want to accidentally hit anyone from LAPD.

"Man down. Something's not right," I shouted into my earplug. "Someone's shooting! I'm not sure where the shots are being fired from!"

Detective Hamilton and his crew rushed forth, swarming the area, and sending retaliatory shots.

"Agent Stamper went that way!" I pointed in the direction of the agent running off. It was so foggy, it was as if Agent Stamper had disappeared into the mist.

Several officers stayed behind to work on Agent Braggs, but I could tell when they stopped, old Glass Eye didn't make it. He was dead.

The old me would have run after Agent Stamper but my baby was beginning to kick like crazy. My doctor had recommended that I stop working at this point to keep from having an early delivery. I had already decided not to take on any more cases, but being arrested gave me no choice. I had to take action. Now I was waist deep in some more corruption. Should I fight or do flight? I didn't know what I was going to do, but it had to be soon.

Chapter Twenty-two

After the smoke and the dust settled, Detective Hamilton came and found me stooping over Agent Braggs's body, both dazed and paralyzed. I couldn't move.

"Are you all right?"

My teeth were chattering; my hands were trembling. I shook my head. "No, I'm not all right. I'm pregnant. I can't be out here fighting. This is the second shootout in a month I've been caught up in."

"You're pregnant?" Detective Hamilton took my hand and helped me stand up. He sounded pleased. "Good. We'll have us a little Romero running around."

I was too numb to respond to that remark. "I'm going to have to get home. Did you find Detective Stamper?"

"No, but we got his number now. We'll pick him up later if he doesn't go on the run."

I took off the wire and handed it to Detective Hamilton. "Can you check the surveillance cameras here and try to see who did the shooting?" I suggested. "The shots came from that direction." I pointed north toward the hazy Santa Monica Mountains, which loomed in the distance.

"Yes, we'll do that. From what the deceased said, there's another blackmailer involved, so that could be the shooter."

How did he know that, then I remembered the wire.

"Anyhow, I think you need to go into protective custody," Detective Hamilton continued. "We're going to need you to testify for us."

"I'll go back home tonight then come back in tomorrow."

"I'll send a police escort with you."

"That's all right. I'll call my sister, Chica. She's a bounty hunter. I will feel safe with her."

I called Chica, and she met me at the house. "I might have to go underground while I testify against this crooked FBI agent."

"You really bite off some big fish, don't you, girl?"

"I know. This thing with my brother's kidnapping was only the tip of the iceberg."

Chica looked down and gently touched my stomach. "How about the baby? Are you going to be all right?" She really looked worried about me.

"According to the doctor, the baby is growing and doing well. This is nothing like how I planned to go through this pregnancy. I'd wanted to have a doula. I'd planned to go to Lamaze and use you as my partner, but none of that is to be."

"Oh, it will be all right." Chica leaned in and hugged me.

"I'm supposed to go in tomorrow and be taken to the safe house."

"Can I do anything?" Chica asked.

"Can you spend the night and take me to wherever I need to be dropped off at so I can leave my car here at the house? Also, can you come check on the house for me?"

"You know I will. Let me call Riley and let him know I'm spending the night with you."

Chica helped me pack a few things, my laptop, my iPad, my camera, and my prenatal vitamins.

I teared up. I didn't know what I was getting into and I didn't know how I'd make it without my friends to help me through this pregnancy.

Chapter Twenty-three

I looked down at my calendar. Last night, Mayhem had gotten back safely from Rio after three months of being out of the country. I didn't even have the heart to ask him what happened. I knew from my experience that, whatever it was, it was one of those things where you'd never be the same after going through it. It was a descent into hell, into the heart of darkness, when you dealt with the cartels in Rio.

I didn't see Mayhem, but I sensed his sadness when we talked over the phone. He said he couldn't find Appolonia. No one would tell him anything and he didn't know if she was dead or alive. I knew that would be some Helen of Troy mess going on if he did find out she was with Diablo aka Escobar.

The next morning, I called Detective Hamilton. "We were able to pick up Agent Stamper at LAX," he said. "Stamper was trying to get out the country. Had his passport and everything. You need to go down to the US Department of Justice to get into a safe house before the trial."

"How long will I have to stay there?"

"I don't know. We'll try to expedite the trial as soon as possible but you know how these things can be."

"Okay." I hung up, feeling totally numb. I knew with lawyers requesting continuances, this thing could go on for a couple of years. What was I going to do?

The US Department of Justice was located downtown on Spring Street and that wasn't far from Silver Lake. I looked it up on the Internet. This was where the witness protection program was housed.

As Chica drove me on the freeway, I was so upset I didn't know what to do. Would I have to change my identity? Would I lose touch with my family, now that I was trying to put my family back together?

I called Shirley from my iPhone. "Shirley, I might have to go underground for a while. Tell everyone I love them."

Shirley sounded upset. "What's going on? I'm really worried about you with this baby. You should be resting while you're pregnant. Your pregnancy is already high risk because of the accident. It's also higher risk at thirty-five. I hope you didn't take on another dangerous case."

"No. This is something that is tied to the last big case, but I'll be fine. The baby is fine. It's kicking and moving all the time." I tried to sound brave, but I was anything but.

Next, I called Venita. I told her that I'd be going underground and to keep Ben indefinitely. "Can you tell Rachel that I'm underground on a big case, but I'll be in touch with her as soon as I get straight? Tell her I won't be calling her for a while."

"Z, I'm really concerned about you. Are you and the baby going to be all right?"

"Just pray for us, Venita," I said, hanging up. I didn't need any more words to upset me.

As we pulled off the freeway at Sixth Street to ride into the heart of downtown, I received a call from Mayhem. I had my Bluetooth on so Chica couldn't hear the conversation. "Sis, what's this about the Brazilian cartel done green-lighted yo' ass?"

"What?" I screamed so loudly, Chica almost ran into the car in front of us. She hit the brakes heavily, just in time.

"What's the matter, *mija*?" Chica asked frantically.

I reached out and touched her. "I'm fine." Then I turned back to my conversation. "When did you find this out? Who told you this?"

"Your boy F-Lock told me. That's the scuttlebutt on the street. I didn't hear nothing about it while I was in Rio. But I did hear you killed four men down there. Baby sis, why didn't you tell me all this shit? Girl, you ain't no joke, is you?" His words were laced with admiration and amazement.

I couldn't even answer Mayhem's remarks.

Mayhem continued, "I have someplace you can hide out while I try to smoke this fool. They call him 'the Executioner.' They say he's one of the best international hit men in the world."

"No, I'm good," I said calmly, but my heart was beating so fast, I thought I would pass out. I did my deep breathing from my tae kwon do teacher and felt myself getting centered.

Lord, what kind of mess had I gotten myself into? Now I must've been crazy. Facing off with the cartel like that. Now they were retaliating. Well, what did I expect? What had I been thinking? But looking back, I was trapped in a corner and it was down to survival of the fittest. And once again, it all came down to dealing with Mayhem. I could strangle him if he were standing near me.

But that was no longer me. That was the me I was before I got pregnant. Now I had a baby to think about. As if the baby heard me, I felt a strong kick.

Don't worry, baby. Mama's going to take care of you—I don't know how, but some way, with God's help, we're going to make it.

Chapter Twenty-four

I stayed at the Department of Justice all day, with only a Subway sandwich and a 7 Up, which they bought for me late in the afternoon. Then, at night, two federal marshals whisked me into a van with blacked-out windows. We drove for about an hour outside the city. I thought we were on the outskirts of L.A. County close to Riverside County.

I was too done in to even worry about the time. I was trying to think of my next move. I planned that I would stay in the program until I had my baby, then I'd move on—where, I didn't know.

"You'll stay here until we get you a more permanent place to stay," the marshal said to me. That was the only information I had.

They took me to a small motel somewhere out in the boonies. The place was called the Starlight Motel, but letters were missing in the marquee. As soon as they opened the door, the place screamed out "second class." The auburn shag carpet on the floor was worn, dirty, and shabby looking. Two white officers were supposed to be guarding me. Both looked unshaven and disheveled. They were not dressed in uniform. They smelled funky, as if they hadn't bathed in days.

"Who are you?"

"That's none of your business," one of the men snapped.

"No, are you the US marshals or the FBI?"

"Don't worry about that. Just know we can keep you safe. I got my friend here."

He touched his .357 Magnum. I didn't feel reassured, seeing as he had liver spots on his hands and hair growing out both ears and his nose. The other man wasn't much more fit, with his rotund belly and balding head, as he touched his Smith & Wesson.

"Do you want Chinese food?" the first man offered.

"No, I'm going to bed." I nodded and went to my room.

From my bedroom, I listened to them play bid whist, pinochle, and Monopoly. I was trying to keep my eyes open because I didn't feel comfortable.

"You want some pizza?" one of the guards asked.

I was so sleepy, I said no. I must have dozed off because a while later, I heard a loud banging sound on the door.

"Who is it?" one of the guards called out.

"Pizza delivery man," a voice called back.

I heard the door open, and a sudden barrage of bullets rang out. I jackknifed up in the bed, frightened. I could hear voices shouting, "Where is she?"

"What are you talking about?" I heard more shots. Through the cracked door I could see blood and gun smoke.

Right away, I knew what time it was. The safe house wasn't safe. I was about to get got. I slipped on my shoes, grabbed my purse, which had my Glock in it, and climbed out the window. I broke into a sprint, then into a fast run. I held my stomach underneath the ridge above my pubic hair. It was damp and cool outside. I felt tall weeds slapping at my legs. I didn't have a coat. I'd left my laptop, my new iPad, and my bag of clothes. I had nothing. Nothing but my will to survive.

I finally came to the bottom of a hill, and found a parking lot nestled in a valley filled with a lot of old-fashioned aluminum-siding trailers. I found one that was empty, a rusted-out trailer down the road but hidden by a willow tree, and I hid there. I was so afraid, I didn't worry about how dank and damp the place felt. I just wanted to go for shelter. I covered myself with old newspaper.

I woke up the next morning not quite sure where I was. I checked around. I touched my stomach and my baby started moving. My stomach growled so loudly, I jumped with a start. I guess the baby and I were both hungry. The sun had come up in the east early. It felt like it was going to be a scorcher. I put my hands over my eyes to block the sun glare, but I could see mountains in the distance off to the North of me. I found my iPhone in my purse and I was grateful. I had nothing else. I only had $20 on me. My driver's license, all my credit cards and debit cards had been taken and I was supposed to be given a new identity, if necessary, by the time the trial took place.

I decided to get moving. I stayed off the road, but close enough to follow the freeway. I was near the Interstate 60. Finally I found an ARCO gas station. I went inside and used the bathroom, then washed up the best I could with paper towel and cold water.

"Where are we?" I asked the store clerk when I came out the bathroom.

"We're in Rialto."

With only $20 to my name, I bought a bottle
of water, a boiled egg, an orange, a banana and
apple, plus a bagel. After I wolfed down the
nourishment, I took my prenatal vitamins.

Now that I had fed myself and my baby, I
could think clearly. I didn't know whom I could
trust. I could only imagine what had happened
to my guards. Obviously, there was a mole who
had leaked my whereabouts. Was there any safe
place for me?

Who could I call, without endangering my
family?

Then I had a thought. I put in a call.

Chapter Twenty-five

Reverend Edgar Broussard pulled up in his church van in front of the ARCO. I had been hiding in the bathroom off and on.

"Thank you for coming," I said as I climbed into the van. I scooted down in the van to hide myself, just in case he was being followed.

"Would you like to come back to my house?"

"No."

"What are you going to do?" He looked down, and noticed I was shivering, teeth chattering. "You don't have a coat."

"I know."

"Here, take my jacket."

Reverend Edgar reached over and slipped his jacket around me. "You're pregnant!" He sounded shocked. That's when I remembered I'd never told him about my pregnancy. "What is going on, Zipporah?"

"If I tell you, a lot of this information could cost you your life. Are you sure you want to know?"

"Please tell me. I can't help you if I don't know what I'm up against."

I let out a deep breath. "Okay. I have to hide out. I was supposed to be going into the witness protection program so I could testify against a corrupt special FBI agent, but the guards were killed at the safe house and I had to escape with my life. Before I left L.A., I found out a hit from Brazil has been put out on my life."

"What?" Reverend Edgar sounded shocked. "How did that happen?"

"I went to Brazil on a case a few months ago, and let's just say I made some enemies there."

Reverend Edgar let out a low whistle. "Okay, Zipporah, you're definitely not an ordinary woman." He shook his head in disbelief. Absently, he ran his hands over his bald head. "I'll tell you what I'll do. I have a cabin up in Big Bear near Seven Oaks that belongs to my family. It's a kind of isolated area. None of my family goes there in the winter so you can be safe. I'll get you a coat and some clothes to make it with. We've also got to buy you some food. There are plenty of blankets at the cabin. I'll come check on you every few days. What are you going to do when it's time to deliver?"

"Well, I've got time. I'll move close to town, or go to a hospital when it gets near my due date."

"I'd like you to take this Bible. You're definitely going to need God's help."

Reverend Edgar stopped and bought me some warm maternity clothes and a wool coat at a general store, which sold everything. We wound up with a cart with what looked like a month's supply of groceries. He made sure I had plenty of vegetables and fruit when I told him I wasn't a big meat eater. He also picked up a blender for me to make a green drink from spinach, chards, ginger root, and kale. I noticed my blood count had gone up since I'd gotten on the green drink. Once we arrived at the cabin, I was pleasantly surprised at how nice and roomy the place was. The cabin was built from dark oak wood with high ceiling beams. A stone-front fireplace with a rocking chair in front of it gave the room a cozy focus.

There were two bedrooms on one floor and one large bedroom in the loft area. The Reverend opened the windows and aired the place out. He showed me the room heaters, which, once they got going, sent a warmth throughout the cabin. He went outside and put a few fresh logs in the fireplace.

The first thing I did was take a long, hot shower. When I came out the shower, wringing out my hair, which was now shoulder-length, I noticed Reverend Edgar staring at me.

I gave him a strange look. "What's the matter?"

He shook his head. "Your hair is beautiful. It has highlights like a raven's wing."

I shrugged. "Thanks."

I felt a little embarrassed, so I pulled my hair back into a ponytail. I'd always had what some Black people called "good hair." My hair had a loose curl in it, and was wavy when it was wet. I didn't wear a press when I was a child. As an adult, I had worn a press or even a perm to try it, but now I was going back to the natural look. Although my hair could look straight with a gel on it, I was glad that the natural hair styles were becoming popular again. I was beginning to think about locking my hair and wearing dreads.

"Do you need anything else?" he asked.

"Well, I hate to be a burden, but I'm going to need to go to an ob-gyn doctor next week."

"We'll find one in a small town near here."

I nodded. As I sat in the rocking chair, I enjoyed the crackling of the logs in the fireplace. For the moment, I was able to put my fears aside.

Meanwhile, Reverend Edgar cooked a nice meal of spaghetti, with dried tomatoes, garlic bread, warm olive oil, and Caesar salad. After he blessed the food, I let out a sigh of satisfaction.

It felt so good to be over the nausea now. Food had taken on a special flavor. I'd never known it to taste so good.

"This is delicious," I said, twirling the pasta around my fork. I dipped the garlic bread into the olive oil. "I'm starving."

"Glad you like it."

"I'm impressed."

"Why?"

"I'm surprised that as a reverend you can cook so well."

"We have to cook at the station during our tour and we take turns. I work forty-eight-hour shifts; then I have four or five days off. I'll be able to come and check on you on my off days, and around my church duties. Are you sure you will be okay?"

"I'll be fine. This will give me time to plan my next move."

"Well, whatever it is, pray about it, and ask for God's guidance."

Generally, I mocked the reverend's talk about God, but now I felt so helpless, so vulnerable, I really knew I had to leave my life in God's hands.

That night, before Reverend left, I asked him about the story of David. "Do you think it was true?"

"What do you mean?"

"That David was able to kill a giant with five stones."

"After David knocked him out with the stones, he took Goliath's sword out of its sheath and stabbed the giant. He also beheaded him once he got him down." He turned away, picked up the Bible, and leafed through it. "Here, you can read the account in the Bible at 1 Samuel 17:40-51."

He opened the Bible and I read it out loud. I couldn't even believe it myself that I was sitting here with a minister, reading from the Bible. "Do you think this was true?"

"Yes, it was a true story. The message is that with God's help, you can fight an army. You know sometimes God sends angels to fight holy wars."

"Well, miracles always happen," I admitted. "I guess it was a miracle how the woman used her car and blocked the other cars when I was hit."

"What woman?" Reverend Edgar looked puzzled.

"The one who kept talking me though while I was trapped in my car. She even called 911. Didn't you see her?"

"No, I didn't see her."

"But she's the one who explained to you what happened."

"I didn't see any woman."

Now it was my turn to be perplexed. "Are you sure?"

"Sure about what?"

A chill sent goose bumps up my arms. "Are you sure you didn't see a woman?"

"No. What did she look like?"

I thought about the scripture about angels coming forth when we didn't even know it. Shirley always said we had guardian angels. I shook that eerie feeling away. "Well, she was a Black woman. She had a calm, soothing voice. Oh, well. I hope I can find her to thank her one day."

I thought of my experience in Rio. I still didn't understand what gave me the strength to do what I did. I felt it was related to the ritual from the Santeria. But, I guessed that was a mystery I would never solve.

Chapter Twenty-six

That first night, I sat down and made a list of what I had to do. I needed to find an ob-gyn doctor in the area and a small hospital where I could deliver in anonymity. I needed to go shopping and buy some yarn—so I could crochet a baby blanket—a wig, and sunglasses for when I went to the doctor. I also decided I would pick up some cloth diapers and a few baby sleepers. I was wondering if I could find some tapes of Lamaze classes on my iPhone, since I thought it might be too risky to go to an outside class. I went on YouTube and found the perfect class.

That first week, the reverend came and took me grocery shopping and we found a small doctor for me to get a checkup. He gave me more prenatal vitamins, when I told him I didn't have the money.

Afterward, we went for a walk by the stream behind the cabin. I picked up five large rocks and had Reverend Edgar tote them back to the cabin for me.

"These are symbolic of the five smooth stones David had," I said. "I'll keep them as a reminder that God is in charge and to help me from being afraid." I put them under my bed for protection.

"That's a good idea. Is there anything I can do for you?"

"Yes, there is."

"Shoot."

"Can you be my Lamaze coach?"

"Sure, but do you think it's safe to go out?"

"Well, they have classes online on YouTube that you can use in the privacy of your home. Do you think you can act as my coach?"

"When do you want to start?"

"We can start now."

I had spread out a blanket on the floor before the fireplace and used four pillows as props. We moved the rocking chair that sat in front of the fireplace out of the way. As Reverend Edgar sat behind me on the pillow, he helped me with the breathing; he was very intense. He gently massaged my shoulders to the rhythm of his voice.

"Pant, pant, breathe," he coached.

Meantime, my mind was on breathing, and all the time I was thinking of Romero . . . how I wished it were him.

Afterward, I noticed Reverend Edgar seemed to be looking pensive. "Are you all right?"

He shook his head. After a while, he spoke, "This reminded me of my wife, Paula, and me." I noticed tears in his eyes. He looked away and wiped his eyes.

I thought about how that had to be the most painful thing in the world—to have carried a baby full term and for it to die during delivery. Worse, his wife had died, taking all their hopes and dreams of building a family life together. I shuddered as a chill ran through me. *Oh, Lord, let me have a safe delivery.*

Impulsively, I reached over and gave him a hug. Before I knew it, Reverend Edgar had embraced me and was trying to kiss me. I didn't want to be rude, but I had never felt any more than a friendship feeling for Reverend. I wasn't over Romero yet, and judging from his tears, he wasn't over Paula.

I slowly eased out of his kiss. "I think it's too soon for both of us. I'm still in love with Romero, even though he's dead."

"I'm still in love with Paula, but I'm sure she would want me to move on, if I found the right woman."

"That would be nice—if you found the right woman."

"I think I have found her."

I stopped in my tracks. Reverend Edgar gave me this strange look, and I recognized it. It was the look that Romero had when he would study me. Oh, no! The Reverend was beginning to catch feelings for me!

"Look, Reverend Edgar," I said, cautiously. "There's a lot you don't know about me. I'm not the right woman for you."

I could see the hurt and embarrassment in his eyes. "Don't say that. You're lovely. You're strong. You're up here, all alone, having your baby by yourself. Don't worry. I won't push you. I know you're still grieving, too."

"I'm glad you understand." An uncomfortable lull fell over the room. Seconds went by but they felt like hours.

I took a deep breath. I tried to reset the energy in the room from this awkward space. "Hey, have I thanked you for all the kind things you have done for me? I really appreciate it. You're one of the good guys."

Reverend Edgar's shoulders relaxed and he looked visibly relieved that I wasn't acting like we could no longer be friends. "I know I'm not your baby's father, and I could never replace him, but how about if I go to the hospital with you when you deliver? I want to be there when you go in delivery."

I hadn't thought about how I would need someone when I went into the delivery room. Then something occurred to me. It didn't matter if the baby wasn't Romero's because Reverend Edgar didn't know what he looked like. I didn't think the minister knew that Romero was a Latino either, because I refused to discuss this with him. And now it didn't matter about the baby's paternity because I knew he or she was mine.

I took a few seconds and thought about it. "Yes, that would be nice. I would be honored to have you go through the delivery with me. That sure would bless my baby." I started laughing. "What better way to enter the world than have a minister present? This baby is going to need it with me as a mother."

Reverend Edgar chuckled, and I could see his mood lift.

Chapter Twenty-seven

I really liked living up on that mountain with its outcropping of rocks, which went up higher behind the cabin. Sometimes I felt like I could go outside and touch the sky, which sometimes shifted from rainforest green to wisteria blue to azure. Sometimes the clouds hung so low, I felt like I was standing in heaven there was such a spiritual vibration here.

A month and a half had gone by and I'd gotten used to living in solitude in the wilderness. Firs, evergreens, and cedars surrounded the cabin. Chrysanthemums, larkspur, morning glories, and late-blooming snapdragons clustered around the yard.

I'd even learned to see in the dark at night. I felt like a panther the way I could see all around without lights on at night.

Often I couldn't get a signal on my cell, but I loved not having distractions. No laptop. No TV. No Facebook, although I could've gotten them on my cell phone or used the computer when I went into town with Reverend Edgar. But I loved this sacred space I was in. It was like a holding pattern in this last trimester.

I chose only to contact the reverend by phone. He said that no one had come looking for me, so I have to assume the Feds thought I just skipped town. I hope they know I had nothing to do with the two officers who were murdered at the safe house. I thought about reaching out to Detective Hamilton to let him know what had happened, but I was too afraid it would endanger his life. Because Romero had always trusted him with his life, I really believed he was clean. Yet, I still couldn't take any chances.

I text messaged Chica so she could tell Shirley and Venita I was safe. For the moment, I wasn't worried about the hit man, or about the blackmailer. I felt free. I felt safe. Life was good.

I went over the series of events. The car accident, the shooting at the cemetery, the shooting at Universal Studios, the shooting at the safe house. Death was all around me, yet I never felt more alive.

Well, DEA Special Agent Braggs had probably been killed from his own blackmailer so that was definitely a case of "Vengeance is mine, saith the Lord." I hadn't had to lift a finger. As far as I knew, FBI Special Agent Stamper was still locked up I knew, but I didn't know who he had paid off, or if they would still try to come after me. I didn't know about the Executioner. Was he still looking for me? I couldn't worry about it.

Instead, I focused on my unborn child. I talked to the baby all the time. This new life was becoming more and more real to me. I felt bonded to the baby. The baby would respond to my voice by kicking. The baby was growing and I was beginning to really stick out. I loved rubbing olive oil on my growing stomach and so far, I didn't have any stretch marks.

The last time Reverend Edgar came to bring food, he remarked, "You're finally growing. I was worried that your baby was going to be too small."

I smiled. "No, it's your good cooking and this mountain air. I stay ravenous. Food has never tasted so good."

I spent most of my time, sitting in the rocking chair, crocheting baby blankets, the craft I'd picked up when I was on bed rest.

On one of the reverend's visits, Reverend Edgar took me to a local doctor, who checked me and said I had a couple more months to go and everything was fine, so I was content. Reverend Edgar even found a secondhand computer at the church; however, I couldn't get the Internet with it. If I wanted to look up anything online, I used my iPhone. It was nice to have something to write on, though. Reverend even bought a journal for me to write in. I recorded my thoughts about the pregnancy, and less and less, I worried about the outside world.

Actually, I was under less stress than when I was in Los Angeles. Birds hung around the cabin and sang at the top of their lungs. I woke up to the sound of blue jays and mockingbirds. Although this was a desolate area, the oak trees had turned a deep sable brown and the leaves were a kaleidoscope burst of gold, umber, burgundy, ochre, and fiery orange and scarlet red. Rhododendron shrubs were in late bloom. I opened my journal and began to write:

I am so happy to wake up here in Big Bear. I'm feeling so uplifted. A deer came to the glass window this morning, wiggled its nose, and it let me know how close I am to nature and to God.

I have always worked and never stopped to take time to see what I was feeling.

This little hiatus in my life has been good.

I dreamed about Romero last night for the first time. He looked really happy. He told me, "I'm fine. You and the baby will be fine."

It seems like the baby even seems at peace here. He moves during the day and not at night.

I'm beginning to think it's going to be a boy. I'm glad I don't know the sex of the baby yet. I'd like to be surprised.

The next morning I woke up to a snow blizzard. I looked out the window and gave out a yell. "I love it!"

Having been raised in Los Angeles, I'd never seen snow up close. I only saw snow on the mountains at a distance. I wasn't a skier so I never had come to Big Bear Mountain.

At first I was excited about the snow. The house felt a little chillier, but I didn't care. I didn't worry about it. I had plenty of water and food. But then I had a weird feel. There was only one way in and one way out just about up here. Reverend Edgar had already been up to visit yesterday and I wondered, could he make it through that snow? I tried to put out a call and couldn't. I couldn't get a signal.

I made a cup of warm cocoa and was reading my Bible, when I felt a gush of water rush down my legs. I wondered, *what was that?* I thought I had urinated on myself. I went to the bathroom and saw what the pregnancy books called "the bloody show."

Oh, no! It was too soon. I wasn't quite thirty-two weeks. I had two more months to go.

I didn't feel any pain, so I didn't know what to do. I tried to call Reverend Edgar again. No signal.

Before I knew it, I doubled over in pain, holding my stomach. "Oh, no, it's not time," I cried out. "God, please help me."

Chapter Twenty-eight

I decided to lie down and pray the pain would go away. Maybe it was what I read about online, Braxton Hicks—false labor. But the pain wouldn't stop. It was as relentless as a hurricane. I started trying to breathe through my mouth like I'd read in the books and seen on the Lamaze videos online. I tried to remember what Reverend Edgar and I had gone over.

Sweat trickled down my forehead and I was huffing and puffing, but I was able to plan in between contractions. I pulled out some scissors to cut the cord. I found thread to tie off the cord. I collected the few baby undershirts, gowns, and cloth diapers I'd been able to buy when I'd gone to the local doctor.

I collected clean sheets and warm blankets. I thought about boiling water, since they always did that in the movies, but I decided to use rubbing alcohol to sterilize the scissors.

"Well, it looks like it's me and you, baby boy or baby girl."

I still didn't know the sex of the baby. I'd seen some Lamaze and childbirth films, and once I was with my old partner, Okamoto, when he delivered a baby in our scout car, but the women generally had a coach and someone helping deliver the baby. Wasn't it dangerous having a baby without a doctor or a doula? Would I die? *Oh, no, if I died, my baby couldn't make it.* I had to make it. I was determined. I tried not to cry out, but as the minutes crept by, my low moans turned to loud groans to loud moans, to animal-like screams. The deep breathing was not helping at all. *Is this what women go through having babies?* I thought through my blaze of pain.

I had never been in so much pain in my life. How could women even live through this type of torture? I almost wished I could die just to stop the pain. I didn't know if I was hallucinating, things felt so crazy. I wondered if this was not a nightmare I couldn't wake up from. Through a foggy mist of blood red pain, I vaguely remember my bowels letting loose and my peeing on myself, but I didn't bother to go to the bathroom. I was afraid I'd deliver the baby into the toilet. When I was on the police force, I'd seen that happen so I didn't want to take chances.

I don't know how many hours went by, but I could tell it was getting dark outside. I had no framework to go by, other than the stages of labor I had learned on YouTube. I cried, I prayed, I hollered during the pains. It didn't feel like no easy stage like they described on the video. How come I couldn't be like the woman who had relatively painless labors, or was that some type of myth? Some of the pains felt like gas pains, some felt like an elephant stomping up and down my spine. I never knew there were so many levels to pain. Pain took on its own music. It was like some dark grotesque threnody which was ancient as the first woman in time, accompanied by my screams. It felt like a demon taunting me.

Finally, after an interminable length of time, I let out one long scream. "Help me, God!" I had one long, excruciating pain and I felt like something split me in half. Then there was another burning sensation, a gurgling plop sound, and then a baby's cry followed. I fell back on the bed, panting. I didn't realize how much I was sweating until I sat up and saw I was soaking wet. I looked down, and there was my baby laying between my legs. It was a girl! And although she looked small, she seemed strong, judging by her lungs. She was as red as a lobster, and not much bigger, but she was beautiful to me. I reached down and

lifted her. I held her close to my breast and let
her nurse. Meantime, she was still connected to
her umbilical cord. Involuntarily, I felt another
push, and the placenta came out.

My bed looked like a massacre had taken place
in it, so I moved over from the bloody/feces/
urine/amniotic fluid area. I decided to lie still
for the moment and get my wits about myself.
I cut the baby's umbilical cord and clamped it
with thread. Instinctively, I pushed my stomach.
There was a gush of blood . . . but it slowed down.
Thank God I wasn't hemorrhaging. I put a towel
between my legs to monitor the bleeding. I swad-
dled the baby in the clean blanket, I changed my
sheets, and I pulled out an old-fashioned quilt,
and covered us both.

I must have dozed off, but when I woke up,
the baby was sleeping peacefully in my arms and
latching on to my breast. She rooted strongly, so
I was glad she was a good feeder. She looked to
weigh about four to five pounds. I unwrapped
her blanket and examined my baby. I counted
all five fingers and five toes and let out a sigh of
relief. I held her up in the light and studied her
as if she was a strange, yet familiar person. It was
as if I'd known her all my life. Her little round
face was framed by a thick crown of straight hair.

"Where have you been all my life?" I sang in my usual off-key voice.

For the first time I took a good look at her face. As tiny as her features were, she looked like Romero! She even resembled his daughter, Bianca. In fact, she looked like the baby picture of Bianca that Romero had once showed me. Her eyes were light hazel when she opened them. "Thank you, Lord!" I said. "You look like your big sister, little one." So I did *get* pregnant on my last night with Romero.

I decided to sit in the rocking chair and rock my daughter for the first time. In the gentle movements, my thoughts raced. For the past twenty-four hour, I had been in an animal-like space. Grunting, bearing down, and having a baby. My body had had a primitive mind of its own. Now, my worries were returning. I was wondering how soon it would be before the reverend came to see me so we could get to a hospital.

I calculated how I would survive. I had enough food for a week, and plenty of water, which reminded me that I was thirsty now. I walked over to the refrigerator and drank a gallon of water. I also fixed a sandwich. I did know with breastfeeding I had to eat. I took my prenatal vitamins. I could make it, I assured myself. The baby had my milk, and I had food. The cabin was warm. The snow had slowed up and I would be all right. I was not bleeding heavily. Each time the baby nursed, I felt my uterus contract, my stomach go down, and the bleeding lessen.

The baby cried only when she was hungry, but overall, she was a good baby. She would nurse, then fall back to sleep. The blizzard had slowed up, but the snow was still falling.

"Angel," I said as I cooed to her in my arms. She grabbed my finger and held onto it. I felt my heart break I was so full with love. "You're a little angel." I'd never fallen so instantly and deeply in love. Then it hit me. I would name her "Angel Romera Soldano-Gonzalez."

Chapter Twenty-nine

I didn't know how long I slept but it was dark outside when I woke up. Shadows shifted up under the door, and I could see the stars through the skylights. The sky was an indigo and periwinkle–looking color tonight. A crescent moon only sent a sliver of light. A haunting wind howled and whistled through the cabin. I was feeling spooked.

I heard someone coming into the cabin. "Is that you, Reverend Edgar?" I called out.

I didn't hear anyone reply. I looked up at a tall, big-boned Black man.

"What do you want?" I asked. My Glock was in my purse, which was near me. *Lord, I will kill anyone who tries to mess with my baby.*

"Miss, I don't want anything. I just need to stay for a minute and catch my breath."

"Who are you?"

"Don't worry. I'm not going to hurt you."

All of a sudden Angel let out a wail.

"Oh, you have a baby?" He lifted his eyebrow in surprise.

I gave him the look that I believed a tigress would send out to any threat to one of her cubs. I pulled my baby close to my chest. I reached for my Glock, which I kept under the pillow next to the wall. I think my intruder saw the fierce look in my eyes because I watched him ease toward the door.

"Don't worry. I'm getting ready to leave. Do you have a car?"

"No."

With that the stranger left as quickly as he came.

I got up and locked the door and put sticks in the windows. *What was that all about?* I wondered.

I thought about how easily this man had slipped into the cabin and it occurred to me that it wouldn't be anything for the hit man to find me up here. I started mapping out my plan. I had to get off this mountain and out of here.

I tried to get a signal on my phone and couldn't. I slept lightly that night. I woke up and fed the baby as needed. I went back to sleep. I think I was dreaming because I heard my deceased father's voice: "Wake up, Z. You've got to be alert. You're the queen now and you've got to protect your castle. You have a baby to protect now."

I instantly woke up. I thought of chess, and how the queen was often used to checkmate the king.

I wrapped up my baby, kissed her, and made her a soft bed of towels, then placed her in a safe corner of the room. I moved the room divider in front of her.

I pulled out my Bible and opened it. I began to pray Psalms 23. "'Yea though I walk through the valley of death, I will fear no evil.'" I rubbed my ankh for extra protection. I knew I was going to need both my Christian and my African mojo to help me.

Suddenly, I heard a slight jiggling of the door. Even with the lock on the door, it slipped open easily. I thought about how easy it was for burglars to get into any house they really wanted to, because that was what they were trained to do— pick locks. It was two in the morning. For some reason, I stayed calm inside. I could hear soft footsteps tiptoeing across the hardwood floor. I knew in my spirit it was "the Executioner."

I had the lights out, but I could quite clearly see the silhouette of a rather tall man with leather gloves and a mask on. He had a 9 mm with a silencer at the end. He was said to be an expert marksman.

"I've been waiting for you," I said softly when he stepped into my room.

I took the first stone and threw it. I missed him. I really don't know what I was thinking; I was hoping to knock him down like David in the Bible. The falling of the stone did alert me to where he was standing because I could hear a "Whoosh" sound from where he was standing.

My would-be assassin aimed to shoot me, but he hesitated when he saw the baby blanket in my arms.

I had wrapped up a towel inside the blanket, put it in my arms, and acted like I had the baby in the bed with me. Seeing what he thought was a baby made the Executioner hesitate—unfortunately, a second too long. Study long, study wrong. I got the drop on him.

I used the wrapped towels with my Glock covered up in it to shoot "the Executioner." The towels were burnt through from the gunfire. I hit him straight between the eyes. *Bull's-eye.*

Once again, it was down to me or him. I hated to kill again, but this time around, I had a child to take care of. I planned to be here to raise my child.

"Miss, did you know the person who was trying to kill you?" The police looked over his pencil as he took the report.

I glanced around the cabin's living room and saw the yellow cordoned-off strip for the crime scene, and the body bag. The room was swarming with deputies and police officers.

"No." I held my face straight. I didn't know who I could trust. I didn't know who was behind killing the guards at the safe house. I didn't know who the mole was, so I had to be careful. Someone had to have leaked that information as to my whereabouts. I glanced over at the Bible sitting in the rocking chair where I last left it after I called the police when I was able to get a signal. I thought about how Lazarus had been resurrected from the grave.

"Lezra de la Croix," I answered.

I remembered how in the movie, *Hurricane*, Denzel, playing as Rubin Carter, said the young boy who found his book, wrote to him, and help eventually get him released from prison was named Lezra, which was a derivative of Lazarus who had been raised from the dead. I guess I was like Lazurus. I'd almost died twice, surely had been spared and I felt as if I was raised from the dead,

The police wrote down the name and didn't ask for ID. "Well, we have a nationwide manhunt going on up here for a police killer. He used to be on the LAPD and was fired. He's gone on a killing spree of police officers and their family. He was last spotted in this area. Have you seen a man who looked like this? His name is Christopher Dorner."

He showed me a picture of a suspect Christopher Dorner. His face looked familiar. I kind of remembered him from when I was on the LAPD. I looked at the picture and shook my head.

But I was lying. I'd seen him before all right. He was the intruder who came in the cabin and left me alone when he saw I was with my baby. I thought about how disenfranchised I felt when I lost my job, but who knew what could make a person crack?

The interviewing officer turned to me. "Well, this looks like this was a professional hit man. He has a passport from Italy. He had a silencer on his gun. You're lucky to be alive."

"Sir, thank you, but I don't know who would do something like this. I had my baby by myself. How soon can you take me to the hospital?"

"I'm sorry, miss, but the roads are kind of shut off. We've got a standoff with the suspect down the road from here. We'll get you out of here as soon as we get the word that this stand-off has come to an end."

Outside I could hear sirens blaring. That was the most noise I'd heard in this isolated place.

I peeked out the window and saw LAPD squad cars, sheriff department cars, CHP, and SWAT teams farther up the hill. Helicopters buzzed around. I could smell smoke and fire, and for a moment, I panicked. I knew when there are fires up in the mountains, people have to evacuate, so what would I do? But then I gave a sigh of relief. Help was here and I'd be able to get to the hospital—eventually.

I went and looked out the window, and saw that the fire seemed to be contained farther up the hill.

I stood up, walked to my bedroom, and picked up my baby, Angel. She was wrapped in a yellow blanket I had crocheted for her. I kissed her all over her soft face. A resplendent sun streamed through the window. For her to be a preemie, the paramedics said she was a healthy baby—no jaundice, no breathing problems. She was already a little blessing.

Out of nowhere, Reverend Edgar came rushing through the front door.

"Zipporah, are you all right?" His face was twisted with agony and worry. "I've been trying to get you on the phone."

He grabbed me and hugged me. Then he looked down and saw baby Angel lying in my arms.

"Are you okay? Wait a minute. What's this?"

"This is my baby."

"What?" he stammered in disbelief. "When did you have the baby? How did you have the baby?"

"She birthed herself," I said simply.

"Oh, my God. I should've never left you here alone. The snowstorm blocked me out, and then this manhunt. But I was able to get through the roads since I came up as a fireman. I had the truck drop me off here. They have law enforcement and fire departments coming in from different counties. It's a media feeding frenzy out there."

"Well, she came early. You had no way of knowing."

Then, Reverend Edgar looked up and saw the body bag and the police standing around taking the police report.

"What happened here?" Looking shocked, he treaded over to the crime scene, trying not to disturb any of the evidence.

The police, who took the homicide report, spoke up to Reverend Edgar. "This is clearly a case of self-defense. Poor defenseless woman with a newborn baby." He clucked his tongue, and shook his head. "I'm so sorry, miss, that you had to go through this."

Reverend Edgar rushed across the room. "You poor baby," he said, hugging me and baby Angel close. "I'll never let you go."

I had to hide my face in his coat collar. I didn't want him to know what I was really thinking. *Poor defenseless woman, my foot!*

In this journey, I had learned that women are much stronger than we think. I thought I would not be able to have a baby as a single parent, but not only did I get through the pregnancy, I delivered her by myself. I hoped I would be a good parent, in spite of all the death threats around me. Angel was my linchpin to love and to life. I didn't love Reverend Edgar, and I didn't think he loved me either, but, I knew he was a good man and had been a good friend to me in a time of need. I had no idea what the future would bring, and at this point, I couldn't worry about it.

Although I never thought I wanted a family, in actuality, I did want a family. That's why I wanted to reunite with my siblings. Now that I was a mother, I felt like I'd come full circle. At first, I felt like I was not the motherly type. But then again, I'd never had a baby, so I didn't know I'd feel such a fierce love. Now, that Angel was here, I felt like a mother, as if I now knew what life was all about. I was happy to have my baby. I was happy that I now had my siblings and my biological mother back in my life too. Most of all, I was grateful that God had brought me through my delivery safely. For now, Baby Angel and I were safe.

I guess love was a funny thing. It came packaged in the strangest ways. I loved my mother, Venita, in one way and I love Shirley aka Moochie in another. Underneath pulling my hair out about Mayhem, I loved my brother. I really loved my newfound sister, Rachel, and was looking forward to meeting my baby brother, Daniel, whom I always loved since I took care of him as a baby. Now that I changed my daughter's diaper, I remember that I changed Diggity's diapers often when he was a baby. I thought having to act as a surrogate mother at the age of eight had turned me against motherhood, but now I saw things differently. It had actually prepared me. I handled my baby with a deftness of an experienced mother.

I had truly loved Romero, and probably always would, but now I had a mother's love for our newborn daughter, Angel.

With the smell of smoke surrounding me, a gunfight with a hunted man raging up the hill from me, I realized something. As fragile, as vulnerable, and as imperfect as we are as human beings, we keep trying to get it right. We keep having children, hoping this time we would do better in the next generation.

Maybe everything happened for a reason. Maybe all the experiences I had gone through, even being born to a Crip mother, was what made me who I was today. I thought about it. What I had gone through had brought me back to God. Now I knew I needed God in my life. And yes, I was bringing Angel into a crazy world, but, as long as there was life, there was hope for a better tomorrow.

The End

Afterword

(instead of a Foreword)

This book is dedicated to all the mothers, who are still living, and who, for whatever reasons, were unable to rear their children. If possible, go back and heal the relationships with your children. It is never too late.

About the Author:

Maxine Thompson is an author of novels, *The Ebony Tree, Hostage of Lies, L.A. Blues, L.A. Blues 2,* and *L.A. Blues 3,* short story collection, *A Place Called Home,* a contributor to anthologies, *Secret Lovers, All in the Family, Never Knew Love Like This, Proverbs for the People,* and editor/contributor to *Saturday Morning.* She also has authored an e book series, *The Hush Hush Secrets of Writing Fiction that Sells, The Hush Hush Secrets of Making Money as a Writer,* and *The Hush Hush Secrets of Creating a Life You Love, 1* and *2.*

She is the host of The Dr. Maxine Thompson Internet show on www.artistfirst.com, the owner of Maxine Thompson's Literary Services and Maxine Thompson's Literary Agency.

She can be reached at:

maxtho@aol.com,
http://www.maxinethompson.com, or
http://www.maxinethompsonbooks.com.

She can be found on Twitter:

@MaxineEThompson

As well as Facebook at Maxine-Thompson.

Readers' Guide

1. If you were in Z's shoes, would you have wanted to have an abortion? Are you pro-life or pro-choice?
2. Why do you think Z changed her mind about the abortion after the car accident?
3. What did you think about the reunion between Z, her long lost sister, Rachel, and her mother? Do you think it was healthy or unhealthy?
4. Does it seem realistic for Z to expect a quiet pregnancy, given her situation with the cartel?
5. Do you think Z was right to help her brother, Mayhem, the kingpin, when he was kidnapped? What would you have done?
6. Do you think Z will have to stay in hiding?
7. Do you think Z should assume a new identity for her and the baby's safety?
8. What did you think of the reality show that Z, her foster sister, Chica, and her friend,

Haviland were starring in? What do you think of reality shows in general?

9. What did you think of the child kidnapping case that Z handled early in the book? Do you think it deepened her commitment to have her child?

10. What did you think of the ordeal that Z went through while delivering her baby?

11. Do you think Z and Reverend Edgar will ever get married? Why or why not?

ORDER FORM
URBAN BOOKS, LLC
97 N18th Street
Wyandanch, NY 11798

Name (please print):_____

Address:_____

City/State:_____

Zip:_____

QTY	TITLES	PRICE

Shipping and handling-add $3.50 for 1st book, then $1.75 for each additional book.
Please send a check payable to:
Urban Books, LLC
Please allow 4-6 weeks for delivery

ORDER FORM
URBAN BOOKS, LLC
97 N18th Street
Wyandanch, NY 11798

Name: (please print):_____

Address:_____

City/State:_____

Zip:_____

QTY	TITLES	PRICE
	16 On The Block	$14.95
	A Girl From Flint	$14.95
	A Pimp's Life	$14.95
	Baltimore Chronicles	$14.95
	Baltimore Chronicles 2	$14.95
	Betrayal	$14.95
	Black Diamond	$14.95

Shipping and handling-add $3.50 for 1st book, then $1.75 for each additional book.
Please send a check payable to:
Urban Books, LLC
Please allow 4-6 weeks for delivery

ORDER FORM
URBAN BOOKS, LLC
97 N18th Street
Wyandanch, NY 11798

Name: (please print):_____

Address:_____

City/State:_____

Zip:_____

QTY	TITLES	PRICE
	Cheesecake And Teardrops	$14.95
	Congratulations	$14.95
	Crazy In Love	$14.95
	Cyber Case	$14.95
	Denim Diaries	$14.95
	Diary Of A Mad First Lady	$14.95
	Diary Of A Stalker	$14.95

Shipping and handling-add $3.50 for 1st book, then $1.75 for each additional book.
Please send a check payable to:
Urban Books, LLC
Please allow 4-6 weeks for delivery

ORDER FORM
URBAN BOOKS, LLC
97 N18th Street
Wyandanch, NY 11798

Name: (please print):_____

Address:_____

City/State:_____

Zip:_____

QTY	TITLES	PRICE
	Diary Of A Street Diva	$14.95
	Diary Of A Young Girl	$14.95
	Dirty Money	$14.95
	Dirty To The Grave	$14.95
	Gunz And Roses	$14.95
	Happily Ever Now	$14.95
	Hell Has No Fury	$14.95

Shipping and handling-add $3.50 for 1st
book, then $1.75 for each additional book.

Please send a check payable to:

Urban Books, LLC

Please allow 4-6 weeks for delivery

ORDER FORM
URBAN BOOKS, LLC
97 N18th Street
Wyandanch, NY 11798

Name: (please print):_____

Address:_____

City/State:_____

Zip:_____

QTY	TITLES	PRICE
	Hush	$14.95
	If It Isn't love	$14.95
	Kiss Kiss Bang Bang	$14.95
	Last Breath	$14.95
	Little Black Girl Lost	$14.95
	Little Black Girl Lost 2	$14.95

Shipping and handling-add $3.50 for 1st book, then $1.75 for each additional book.
Please send a check payable to:
Urban Books, LLC
Please allow 4-6 weeks for delivery